ANYTHING FOR HIM

MORE THAN ANYTHING 2

TT KOVE

ARCTIC CIRCLE PRESS

PART I
THE MORE THINGS CHANGE

GEIR

*D*ad and I didn't drive straight to Oslo, but took frequent stops to stretch our legs and to eat.

We even booked into a hotel for the night.

There were about another three hours of driving left, but Dad was tired and he didn't want to drive when he was. I could understand that. Most vehicular accidents happened when the driver was tired, after all, or so the statistics said.

Dad got us a single room with two beds.

After dropping off bags, we headed down to the hotel's restaurant.

A young, bubbly waiter, who, quite honestly, was rather handsome, sat us at our table and handed us menus.

"Find anything interesting?" Dad asked.

We hadn't talked much in the car. He'd been focused on the road, and I'd been sullen and upset, wondering if I'd done the right thing when I'd asked Uncle Daniel to be there, so he could talk to Jørgen once I'd left.

Jørgen had seemed to take me leaving okay when I was there, but I wasn't so sure he would once I was gone.

So I'd asked Uncle to talk to him.

I hoped it had all turned out okay, that it wouldn't all blow up in my face. Or Jørgen's, rather, considering how he reacted to therapists in general.

"I don't know." I started paying attention to the menu. The words had faded earlier, because my thoughts had been other places, but now I found I managed to focus.

"I'm thinking a nice, big steak would taste good."

I made a noncommittal sound.

Steak was my dad's favourite, but I wasn't much keen on it. Chicken breasts, maybe, or a hamburger. They also had a good selection of various pasta dishes, but I didn't feel like pasta.

"I'll have the chicken breasts in a spiced tomato cream sauce. With chips on the side, instead of baked potatoes."

"That sounds good." Dad smiled tentatively at

me. He'd been hesitant with me ever since we'd left. Maybe because I'd been crying for the first hour and silent and sullen for the next five. "Can I ask you something?"

"Sure." But if he was going to say something about Jørgen, about our relationship, the he could sod off. I didn't need to hear how he thought Jørgen was too old for me.

"Why did you ask Daniel to take time off from work to be there when we left? He told me you had asked him to be there, but he didn't say anything else. I'm just curious, considering you didn't ask Carina or Marika to stop by too."

I stared down at the wooden tabletop. "I wanted him to be there after we left. Jørgen... I didn't know how Jørgen would take it."

"He seemed to take it better than you."

"Yeah. Because I was there. But when we left, I wasn't sure what would happen. Since Uncle's a psychiatrist, I asked him to be there to talk to him if he took it badly."

"I'm sorry to say this, but he seems to have a lot of issues. Why isn't he in therapy already?"

I knew Dad didn't mean anything bad, but I bristled at the question. "He has his reasons. I don't know what they are, but I can guess. He doesn't want to talk about his previous therapist, exactly like he shuts down whenever an uncle of his is mentioned."

Dad rested his elbows on the table and crossed his hands. He stared at the tabletop now too. "Something bad has happened to him in the past?"

"Something really bad. Something that leaves him with severe anxiety. He has flashbacks and panic attacks, and only the smallest touch can set it off." I wasn't sure Jørgen would like me talking about him and his issues, but I needed to talk to someone, and my dad was the only one I had right now.

He was the only one I could talk to, besides Jørgen himself. And maybe if he knew some of what Jørgen went through on a day to day basis, Dad would be more sympathetic towards him.

"And even with all this…" Dad motioned slightly with one hand. "You still like him? You still want to be with him?"

I nodded fiercely. "Jørgen might have issues, but they don't define him. He's compassionate, he's kind, and he cares about me. When I rang him up, that day with Charo, it was only around noon and he came rushing over from *work*. All he's ever done is care about me. And I think being with me has made him better, too. In the beginning, I couldn't even touch him without him jerking away from me."

The waiter appeared again to take our order.

"I'm sorry, Geir," Dad said once the waiter walked away. "I'm sorry for forcing you to move away from someone you obviously care a great deal about. I honestly thought it would be good for you, though. Charlotte and I talked about them moving in with us, you know. We figured that my house was too small, and I figured you wouldn't mind moving, since you didn't have any friends."

He sighed. "I should've asked you first, before Charlotte and I made our decision. I didn't know about Jørgen, and maybe if I had known beforehand things would've turned out differently, but now..." He shrugged awkwardly. "I'm sorry."

"It's okay, Dad." It wasn't really, but I understood his reasoning. He'd done what he thought was best for me, which was to move away so I could get away from the lonely life I'd led. And perhaps make proper friends someplace new.

I reached into my pocket to withdraw the note Jørgen had given me.

"What's that?"

"Jørgen gave it to me, before we left." I unfolded the note. "It's the number for Tarjei's little brother, Nikolai. Tarjei is his best friend. He said Nikolai's moving to Oslo to study, and that I should ring him up."

"That was nice of him. To give you his number, I

mean." Dad steepled his fingers together. "You should give him a call once we're settled. Maybe you'll hit it off, huh? Wouldn't that be nice?"

"I don't know…"

"You don't know? Why?"

"Like, what would I say? *Hey, Jørgen gave me your number, and it would be cool if we could meet up*?"

"That's a good way to phrase it."

"It sounds so lame." I fingered the note.

I wondered what Tarjei's brother was like. I had only met Tarjei a couple of times, but he was a nice bloke. He didn't match Jørgen at all in personality—in fact they were exact opposites—but they kind of fit. I wondered if Tarjei's brother would be like him. If he was, I'd probably like him. He'd probably be open to new friends too, because Tarjei struck me every time as a very open, social, and welcoming person.

But that was a very big *if*.

His brother could be totally different.

"I'll think about it."

"I think you should definitely do it. He can't be so bad if Jørgen gave you his number, could he?" Dad smiled slightly.

Our drinks arrived.

"Have you met him before, this Nikolai?"

I shook my head. "I have no idea who he is." But

then I didn't know anybody, did I? I only knew who my classmates were. Nikolai could've gone to my school, but he could've also gone to the general studies school. "Jørgen said he was moving to Oslo to study at a dance academy."

"Dance?" Dad's eyebrows rose.

"Yeah. Blokes can dance too, you know."

"Yes, of course." Dad shook his head slightly. "Of course, I didn't mean anything by it. It just surprised me, is all. After all, how many blokes do you hear about that actually want to study dance?"

I shrugged my shoulders. "I don't know. I don't know any blokes period."

"The one in your class. The one who punched you…" Dad's gaze settled on my eye, the one that'd taken Jonas' hit a while ago. There was no trace of the shiner anymore. "Did you make up with him before school was over?"

"Make up with him? It wasn't like we ever fell out. He just never liked me, and he wasn't shy about expressing it." I wrapped my hands around my water and took a big sip. "So no, I didn't make up with him. Frankly, if I'm happy about anything right now it's that I don't ever have to deal with him again."

"Do you know why he didn't like you?"

"Don't know. I think, at first, it might be

because of my epilepsy. He kept calling me freak and all that, you know. Then when he found out I was gay he started in with the homophobic slurs. I generally ignored him, but it was difficult the times he tripped me or shoved me into stuff. That time I snapped back... that's when he hit me."

"If something like that happens in your new school, you come tell me. I won't tolerate that kind of behaviour towards you. I won't."

Dad seemed so determined I had to smile.

"I hope it won't come to it, though."

New city, new school, a whole set of new people... I didn't think I'd get along great with everyone in my new class, because how realistic was that? But I hoped to at least get on friendly terms with some of them.

I didn't want to spend another year in school being called names and shoved into things. I'd even take being ignored in front of that, though I'd very much prefer if that didn't happen either.

Like I'd told Jørgen those months ago: all I wanted was a friend.

I wasn't expecting much—just one would do. One friend, and I would be happy.

And during the holidays I'd go back home and spend time with Jørgen. If I could spend all the four holidays during the school term with him, then next summer wasn't all that far off, was it?

I was going to keep thinking like that.

Keep being positive.

Positive thinking, that's what I was going to be all about from now on.

DAD and I got up early the next morning.

Neither of us had any particular need to linger in the hotel, even if it was a nice one, so we got on the road early.

That also meant we arrived early.

The clock was nearing two when Dad swung the car into a gravelled driveway and parked it next to a silver one.

I got out of the car and stared up at the big house. It was painted white and had black shutters. There were curtains and flowers in every window I could see. It looked downright cosy and inviting.

"Do you like it?" Dad came around to stand beside me. He put a hand on my shoulder and squeezed slightly as he too looked up at the house.

"I do. It looks nice."

"Let's head inside and greet Charlotte before we start carrying our stuff in." Dad nodded across the lawn, where four stairs led up to a veranda and the front door.

Dad's hand dropped from my shoulder as we crossed the driveway and continued across the lawn.

The front door opened ahead of us and Charlotte stepped out, a big smile on her face as she waved.

Dad waved back at her and quickened his steps. He took the stairs in two jumps and embraced her in a tight hug.

I grinned to myself, glad to see Dad so happy. For years now Dad had been all about making life better and more comfortable for us, and that had meant his life had been all about work.

I'd put one foot on the first step when the aura hit me.

I managed to retract that step before I was swallowed by the darkness.

$\mathcal{I}$ woke up feeling sore and groggy, with a plain, white ceiling far above me.

Blinking myself into awareness, I slowly turned my head. I was in a strange room. One that was empty save for the bed I was lying on. The room was also painted white, the exact same shade as the ceiling.

Pushing myself up on my elbows, I saw my bag on the floor, next to the bed. The zipper was undone. I pushed my quilt down and saw that I was in a completely different set of clothes than I'd been in on our drive.

In fact, I was in comfortable jogging bottoms and a T-shirt.

Oh no.

A change of clothes could only mean one thing.

I staggered a couple of steps as I surged out of bed. My head felt heavy, like I'd taken a hit to it, which I probably had. I'd been on the lawn, thankfully, and not on the gravel driveway or on the stairs.

My groggy head didn't stop me from feeling mortified. *Way to make a first impression.* Not only had I had a seizure, but my bladder had decided to take a holiday during it.

Walking out of the room, I couldn't see anyone—couldn't even hear anyone—but I could smell food. Had they eaten without me?

What was the time, even?

I doubled back into what I supposed was my room to gather my mobile from atop my bag. It was a bit before eight. Mystery solved; I'd been asleep almost six hours.

I went downstairs, and the smell of food led me into a spacious kitchen. Charlotte stood at the counter, stirring something in a stock pot.

She must've heard me come in, because she turned to me with that ever-present smile. "Are you feeling all right?"

I couldn't meet her eyes. "A little groggy, but fine, yeah."

"Good." She turned back to stirring. "I'm making

lasagne. Your dad said it was one of your favourite dishes?"

"It is." I gravitated closer to her.

"Yngvar went out to buy garlic bread."

"Oh." *Now we're talking.* "I'm sorry about earlier," I mumbled. "I'm in new clothes, so I guess I—I mean, did I—?" My face burned in embarrassment and I bowed it so she couldn't see.

"Your dad carried you up to bed and changed your clothes." There was no judgement in her tone that I could detect.

Her words only mortified me more, however. Dad had done it my entire life, but I was seventeen now, and the thought of Dad seeing me naked... I shuddered. The other possibility wasn't exactly ideal either.

"Don't fret about it. I knew you had epilepsy, your dad has told me all about it. So don't be embarrassed that you had a seizure. There's nothing to be embarrassed about."

There was plenty to be embarrassed about, but I didn't say that. I was lucky that every time I'd had a seizure around Jørgen, I had remained dry. How mortifying wouldn't it be if the bloke I was in love with found me seizing and drenched in urine?

"Do I have time to take a shower?" I looked into

the stock pot. The lasagne filling was bubbling slightly.

"You do. I haven't even filled the roaster or put it in the oven. It's supposed to be in for fifty minutes, so use your time."

I backtracked out of the kitchen, then stopped.

"Um, where is the bathroom?"

"Upstairs, at the end of the hall, three doors away from your room." Charlotte turned to look at me again. "There are towels in the tall cabinet next to the sink. If you haven't got shampoo or soap yet, you can use whatever's in the shower. We won't mind."

"Thank you." I gave her a slight smile, then slipped out of the kitchen to go back upstairs.

I had shampoo and shower gel in my bag, and I gathered that as well as a new set of underwear, jogging bottoms, and a T-shirt. Dad might've changed me, but there must still be urine on my skin. I couldn't imagine he'd washed me. Dried me, certainly, but not washed me. Not anymore.

I preferred to do the washing myself, thank you very much.

The shower was floor-level, unlike the one we'd had which had been a stall shower. It had big glass doors with small round handles on both sides so that it could be opened from both the inside and outside. The floor was nice and warm thanks to cables, so it wasn't a shock in temperature to shuck my clothes.

Since Charlotte had told me to, I did take my time.

I shampooed and washed properly, making sure to scrub myself so I was certain the urine would rinse off. I hated when I pissed myself during a seizure. *Especially* when it happened at school.

I close my eyes against the water. I hoped I wouldn't get such seizures when I started school now. Not until I'd got to know someone, anyway. I knew I couldn't control it, but I hoped my introduction to the class wouldn't involve a seizure at all, least of all one where I wet myself.

The big mirror over the sink was fogged over when I finally shut the shower off. I dried myself quickly and dressed, then wiped the mirror off so I could look at myself.

I ran the towel over my hair so water wouldn't drip on my clothes. My hair was getting a bit long, but I kind of liked that it fell around my face.

I fingered the yin-yang necklace adorning my neck.

I already missed Jørgen like mad, but did I dare ring him? What if he was angry with me for asking Uncle to talk to him?

I reached for my mobile and fiddled with it. I

wanted to talk to him, but I was unsure of the reception I'd get.

Jørgen didn't like therapists.

What if me asking Uncle to talk to him had made Jørgen's anxiety worse?

I bit down on my lower lip, then unlocked the screen and clicked on my recent calls. Jørgen's name stood out from the rest, which were only Dad and the rest of the family.

I pressed his name with my finger quickly, before I could change my mind. I sank down atop the toilet while I waited for it to connect.

"Hey." Jørgen answered on the fifth ring. I couldn't gauge his mood from that simple word.

"Hey," I replied, my throat thick.

"Are you all right?"

"Are you?"

He was silent for a moment. "Daniel said you'd asked him to talk to me."

"Are you angry?" I grabbed my mobile tight. "I can understand that you would be, really, I can, but I was worried about you and I just… He was the only one I could ask."

"It's okay," Jørgen said softly. "We actually had a, uh, nice chat."

Really? "I'm happy to hear that." I truly was. I

wanted to ask if he'd keep seeing Uncle, but I didn't know how to form the question.

"I'm going back to therapy." It was said quickly, determinedly, but I could hear the slight catch in his voice at the end.

"You're going to keep seeing Uncle?" I was surprised. It was a good kind of surprised, though. He, who had been so against therapy before—or at lest had some and memories from it—was now going to go back to it? I hadn't thought it would be this easy.

"Well, yeah, I guess. In the beginning, at least. But I'm going to see someone else too. He's going to help me find someone eligible. Preferably a woman." I could tell Jørgen was getting agitated by the subject.

"I'm glad," I whispered.

I was happy he was finally getting help. He needed it. He needed to work through whatever happened to him in his past, instead of pushing it away. Because that didn't seem to be helping him at all. I wasn't sure if I'd been of any help or if I'd made it worse. I'd been of help when it came to the touching, certainly, because he could stand that now. But as for the rest…

He couldn't sleep when I spent the night, and if he did, it was a restless sleep and he woke every time I moved. Maybe he was like that when he was alone too, but he was quite vague about it whenever I asked, so I had no idea.

"So are you doing all right?" He changed the subject to me, and I let him. I'd pushed him enough in the past days, with Uncle and my questions now.

"Yeah. We got here early today, but I had a seizure, so I've been sleeping since."

"Are you hurt?"

"No. No, I'm not." If Charo had been there, he would've got in-between my head and the ground, so that I wouldn't be hurt. But as Charo wasn't here anymore...

"Good." I could tell he was relieved just from that single word.

He worried about me, and that made me feel good.

I worried about him too, though, and I probably had more reason to worry about him than he had about me.

"I miss you," I said quietly. I wished I could spend my evening with him, eating lasagne and garlic baguettes in his flat. I just wanted to be around him. He made me feel good about myself, even if we didn't touch. Just being in his presence did it, and I already missed him so much.

"I miss you too." His voice was so low I had to strain to hear it—but I did.

The autumn holiday was too far away.

I had the whole summer to get through, as well as half the school semester. Why did Dad have to leave the moment school let out?

I bowed my head slightly to stare at my discarded towel on the floor. We'd left early because Dad had his three weeks off now, then he'd take his holiday after. He wanted to stay home for as long as possible so the both of us could adapt well to our new living situation.

I understood that, I did, but that didn't make me miss Jørgen any less or make me stop wishing to spend my time with him instead of being where I was.

"I have to go. Charlotte's making my favourite for dinner." I didn't want to go downstairs—I wanted to stay right where I was, talking to him. "It was nice talking to you, Jørgen. Hearing your voice."

"Yeah." He sighed, and I wondered if he felt the same way I did. If he missed me just as much as I missed him and if he wished I was there with him instead of here.

I hoped he did.

We said goodbye, and I sat clutching my phone for a whole minute. I closed my eyes and breathed deeply.

It hadn't been the most fulfilling conversation.

I hoped he wasn't shutting me out.

I cleaned up after myself and dropped my old clothes next to my bag. Charlotte wasn't in the kitchen anymore when I came downstairs, but I found her in the dining room, where the table was set. They were all there: Charlotte, Dad, and two people who could only be Charlotte's kids.

Dad spotted me first. "What took you so long?"

I stared at the floor. "I was talking to Jørgen."

"Are you all right?" Dad asked, more tentative now. He tended to sound like that when it came to Jørgen.

"Yeah. Why wouldn't I be?"

He shook his head. "I was just wondering. You seem a bit subdued."

"Because I miss him."

"Sit down, Geir." Charlotte motioned towards the table, where her two children were already seated on the opposite end of where I was standing. She took the seat at the head of the table, and I sat down next to Dad.

I looked over at the two across me. The girl looked back, seemingly friendly, which was nice, while the boy seemed completely uninterested. I wasn't sure if it was an attitude towards me in particular or his attitude in general, which left me a bit hesitant.

"Hi." The girl reached a hand across. "I'm Marlene. It's so nice to finally meet you. We've heard so much about you." She had her mum's smile and blonde hair. "This is Kristoffer. He's sulking because he wasn't allowed to go hang out with his mates tonight." She elbowed her little brother and he glared at her.

"I am *not* sulking." It didn't sound very convincing.

Where Marlene was a mirror image of Charlotte, Kristoffer was the opposite. He was dark haired, so he must look like his dad.

"You're not helping your case." Marlene turned back to me. "Mum said you had a seizure once you got here. Bummer, that. But at least you're up now for dinner, huh? Would've sucked to miss being introduced to us all, now, wouldn't it?"

I chuckled, a bit uncomfortable. I didn't know what to say to that. She seemed nice, but the embarrassment of the seizure was still weighing me down. At least it didn't seem Charlotte had told her *everything*. If she had, I might've simply died from humiliation right there.

"How was Jørgen doing?" Dad asked. I turned my head towards him. He wasn't looking at me, but down at his plate. I wondered if he was genuinely curious or simply trying to strike up a conversation with me.

"Fine. He was doing fine."

Charlotte motioned for me to fill my plate first, and I cut off a square piece of the lasagne to load on my plate.

"With Daniel, and everything…?"

"I think he was grateful about that, actually." At least it had got him to decide to go back to therapy. I hoped it helped. I hoped it helped with all my heart.

I grabbed a garlic baguette from a plate next to the lasagne.

"Who's Jørgen?" Marlene looked at me curiously. "A friend of yours?"

"Boyfriend," I said immediately. I might be in a new city, far away from home, but I wasn't about to hide what Jørgen was to me. I wasn't about to hide *who* I was.

"Aww." Marlene looked at me kindly, which drew me up short for a moment. "Sucks that you had to leave him behind. That's sad." She seemed completely sincere.

"Yeah," I replied dazedly. "Yeah, it is." I noticed Kristoffer glancing at me, but when he saw that I'd noticed, he quickly turned to filling up his own plate.

"I thought we could go to Ikea tomorrow." Dad leaned closer to me as he reached for a garlic baguette. "Since we aren't getting our furniture shipped, we need to buy you some new stuff."

"If you don't like the bed in your room, feel free to change it out," Charlotte said. "It's an old bed, but I put it in there so you'd have something to sleep on until you bought something else."

"Thanks." I smiled at her before turning to face Dad. "Can I get paints and stuff?" We'd used to paint at school, but as I was now going to be doing general studies, I wouldn't have that opportunity anymore.

"What does that entail?"

"Easel, canvases, palette. Paints, obviously."

Dad looked at me. "I thought you preferred to draw?"

"I do. But I like painting too, and as my arts education is done…" I shrugged.

"Sure, we'll find that tomorrow as well."

I cut up my lasagne in pieces so it would cool down a bit faster, then fiddled with my mobile while I waited.

I should send Nikolai a text. I didn't think I'd be brave enough to ring him, but texting was fine.

Wasn't it?

"Uh, Dad," I said quietly, realising something, "my jeans… Where are they?"

"I threw them in the hamper. Charlotte said she was going to put a load in the washer later tonight."

Shit. The note with Nikolai's number was in a pocket of those jeans. I'd have to retrieve it after dinner, before Charlotte did laundry.

Better yet, I would write the number down on a new piece of paper because the old one wouldn't be dry.

I could leave it, but I actually did want to text Nikolai. Even if the simple thought of reaching out like that to someone else left me short-breathed and with sweaty palms.

But look where reaching out to Jørgen had got me.

I hoped, *really* hoped, that I wouldn't regret it.

CHAPTER 3

I stood outside Oslo S, bouncing on the balls of my feet in nervousness. I had my mobile in one hand and I kept checking the time. I was early, but I'd rather take an earlier train into Oslo central than be late.

Being late would not make for a good first impression.

I'd contacted Nikolai the day after I'd arrived in Oslo, like I'd told myself I would. He'd replied, very kind and optimistic, but he hadn't actually moved down to Oslo yet.

Now, two weeks later, I was meeting him for the very first time in person. I had no idea what to expect; I didn't even know what he looked like.

It dawned on me that meeting in front of Oslo S

wasn't the best place when you didn't know what that someone looked like. There were a *lot* of people milling around me, going here and there. Some lounging, some immersed in their phones, others running to reach the trams or the busses.

"Geir?"

I jumped in surprise, then quickly turned around.

"Nikolai?"

I was a bit taller than him, which was a shock in itself because I wasn't the tallest person around. However, his outfit outdid any shock about something as trivial as height.

He wore a black jumper, which was unzipped, showing off the vest underneath. The vest was loose over the chest with *My boyfriend's hotter than your boyfriend* in rainbow letters. His jeans were loose-fitting and wine-red, and he wore a rainbow belt around his hips, though I didn't think it helped keep the jeans up. His Converse were obviously well-worn, but the baby-pink colour couldn't be missed.

"The one and only."

He held his arms out to the side, and I could see that they were adorned with bracelets in all kinds of colours. His eyes were brown and seemed to sparkle, his hair auburn and shaved short on the sides while it was long on top.

He was gay with a capital G.

He was the most out and proud person I'd ever seen.

I couldn't remember ever seeing him back home, which was weird, because I would've remembered him if he always dressed like this.

"How'd you know it was me?" I asked.

"Tarjei described you to me." Nikolai looked me up and down with a wry tilt of his lips. "Young, blond, cute, innocent. Jørgen's type, apparently, though I didn't even know Jørgen had a type, you know?"

He was like those stereotypical gay men more often than not portrayed on television. He even had the so-called limp wrist.

I found I didn't mind one bit.

He was out and he was proud, and I *liked* it.

I admired it.

He wasn't afraid to show who he was—in fact, he shoved it in people's faces.

"It's nice to meet you," I finally managed, hoping he didn't think I was being rude.

"Right back at you." He moved in to kiss my cheek instead of shaking my hand, like I was used to and had expected. "And call me Nik. Everyone does." He shrugged his thin shoulders. The muscles stretched tight under the skin. If he was a dancer, he must be in good physical shape. "So what do you want to do? Are you hungry?"

"I guess, yeah." It'd been a while since breakfast. I'd got up early, too nervous to stay in bed any longer.

"Want to head down to T.G.I. Fridays?" He nodded his head to the right. "I know there's one right here, but I prefer the one on Aker Brygge. It's not that long a walk, but we could take the tram or a bus, if you're not up for it."

"I don't mind walking." And so we headed up Karl Johan, the designated shopping street of Oslo city centre. I'd already been there a couple times since I'd arrived in Oslo.

Everything was so much bigger than I was used to, but there were also a lot more shops than we had back home. There were a lot of the same chain shops, but the shops here were bigger and had more to choose from.

I couldn't help but like it, even if I missed home like mad.

Missed Jørgen most of all.

"So how'd you hook up with Jørgen?" Nik asked. "I don't mean to be, like, nosy, but I'd never expected Jørgen to actually meet someone."

My heart skipped a beat. "You know Jørgen?"

"Nah." He shook his head and grinned. "He's Tarjei's mate. Tarjei needs someone to talk to sometimes, though, and more often than not that someone tends to be me. Besides, I've been there through it all, right? I know about Jørgen, which is why I never thought he'd meet anyone. Too damaged, you know?"

I nodded. I reckoned that meant Nik knew more than I did.

I didn't really know anything at all, did I?

Jørgen didn't speak about his past, and what I'd guessed… it didn't have to be true. Though I was pretty certain about that uncle.

"So?" Nik looked at me inquiringly.

"So what?" I blinked.

"So how'd you hook up with Jørgen?"

"Oh. Well, we didn't hook up, really. He helped me when I had a seizure."

"Seizure?" It was Nik's turn to be confused. So Tarjei hadn't told him that part about me? Maybe Jørgen hadn't told *him*.

"I have epilepsy."

"What, really? Like, full on jerking on the ground?" Nikolai seemed more fascinated than disgusted, which was a new thing for me.

"Yeah." I couldn't help but chuckle at his description of it. "It's called tonic-clonic seizures, though.

Used to be called grand mal, if you've heard about that?"

"It rings a bell." Nik tapped a finger to the side of his head. "So he helped you when you had a seizure. How'd you get from that to being, like, his boyfriend?"

"We started out as friends and it just... it just happened, I guess." I fingered my necklace. We'd shared our first kiss after he'd given me that.

"That's nice." Nik's eyes focused on my throat. On the necklace. "Special gift from someone?" Now his eyes were really sparkling.

"From Jørgen, yeah." I blushed slightly.

Nik laughed. "You're cute. I can see what Jørgen sees in you. Tarjei was right, you're all sweet and innocent."

I wasn't sure I liked that description of me. Sweet and innocent? Still, at the same time it was nice to hear. I'd been judged all my life because of my epilepsy, and I'd take anything nice and cling to it.

"So why're you in Oslo? Why aren't you back home with Jørgen?"

"Dad's got a girlfriend here and they decided to move in together." I was only a little bitter about that now. I was happy for Dad. And Charlotte. If I wished I could be somewhere else... well. I didn't have any other choice at the moment. "So here I am."

Nik grimaced. "Sucks, that."

"Yeah, it does," I replied quietly. "Do you know anyone down here?"

"Nah." He made a movement with his hand. "I'll get to know people once school starts. Or when I go out clubbing. And now I know you!" He grinned at me.

I smiled back. "Yeah."

Nikolai was *fun*.

He was himself to the fullest and he didn't care that some people threw him long looks. He talked constantly and laughed often; he was lively and constantly in a good mood, as well as always positive and optimistic.

We sat at a table on T.G.I. Fridays for hours, just getting to know each other.

I wished I could've met Nik when I lived back home. He was very sociable. It wouldn't have done anything for my situation at school, Jonas would've still been an idiot, but I could take whatever people had to dish just to have one friend.

"So what did you study back home?" Nik asked me, his full focus on me as he waited for the answer to his question.

"Arts," I said, eating the last of my chips. We'd both gone for hamburgers and we'd devoured them in no time. "That's only two years, so now I'm doing a year of general studies."

Nik made another grimace. "Sometimes I wish I'd gone to vocational school. I did the music, dance, and drama line, choosing dance, obviously, but we still had to go three years and do tons of general studies. Both Ben and I, my best mate, Jørgen's cousin, hate general studies, but I wanted to do dance and he wanted to do music. There wasn't anything vocational we wanted to do." He shrugged. "I can't understand how you'd willingly do an entire year of just general studies."

"I don't know what else to do, so it's better than nothing. Besides, it gives me the opportunity to apply to university if I want to."

"Well, that's true." Nik bobbed his head. "I could go to university too, but I want to continue dancing, so I decided to go to the Bårdar Academy. They're extremely good and we have to do a lot of different dancing as well, so it's quite versatile." He pursed his lips. "Ben, on the other hand, doesn't know what to do now, so he's getting a job. He likes music, but he's not very good at studies in general. He's got dyslexia."

"How long have you been friends?"

"Since forever." Nik chuckled. "We met first day in first grade and have been best friends since."

"That must be nice. To have had such a good friend with you for so long."

"It has its ups and downs. We're totally different people, so we can get into the most ridiculous fights. We always make up again, though." Nikolai leaned forward a bit and crossed his arms on the table. His vest, which was already loose around the chest area, fell down to reveal a flat, hairless chest and… pierced nipples.

I couldn't help but stare.

Nik caught me because he looked down at himself. "Like them, do you?" He grinned wickedly.

"I… That must've *hurt*." There were identical silver bars through both nipples. I winced just thinking about it.

Nik laughed. "Not really. Besides, any discomfort I had when I first got them is now forgotten because they feel so bloody *good*. Like, they make my nipples even more sensitive. I have my navel pierced too. That's only for vanity, though. You should see Ben; he's got his cock pierced."

My eyebrows rose in surprise at that. My wince was even more pronounced now. Nipples, all right, a lot of people pierced them, but piercing your dick… wow. That must *really* hurt.

Nik continued laughing. "You should see your

face. It's priceless. I take it you're not a fan of piercings?"

I shook my head slowly. "Never given them much thought. I don't think I'd ever want to have one, though."

"Not even in your tongue?" Nik's tongue came out to wet his lip, then he took the round silver bar between his teeth to play with it. "I tell you, blokes love it when you've got a tongue piercing. It feels amazing when you go down on them."

I couldn't help the blush that crept up my neck and bled into my cheeks.

Nik stared at me for a long moment. "You've never gone down on—?"

I shook my head quickly, not wanting him to finish the sentence. It was too embarrassing. "No, never."

"But… you and Jørgen—?" He seemed to be lost for words.

"We've never done anything."

"Well, okay, I can see that. Jørgen's got, like, a ton of issues. But you haven't with anyone else either?"

When I simply shook my head again, he sat back in his chair to stare at me. "Ahh, mate, you're missing out! There's nothing better than banging a hot bloke."

"I wouldn't know." I could still feel that my cheeks were red.

"How could you be a virgin? You're adorable. I bet blokes would stand in queue to bang you."

I snorted. "Hardly."

He cocked his head. "Does the epilepsy make problems for you? I don't know anything about epilepsy, so sorry if I'm all wrong."

"No. Well, yes, kind of. Not the epilepsy itself, but the medication. I don't know, really. I've been on medication since I was little. I'm not sure if the lack of a, uh, sex drive is simply the way I am or if it's because of the medication."

"Huh." He crossed his arms over his chest. "You should figure that out, because mate, *sex*." He said it like it was supposed to mean everything.

For him, it probably did.

For me, not so much.

I didn't know what I was missing out on, so I couldn't exactly miss it, could I?

I wasn't quite sure how the conversation had ended up on such a private subject as sex. We'd only just met, yet now he knew my sexual history. Or rather, my lack of one.

He was easy to talk to, granted, and he wasn't judging me. He was simply surprised.

I reckoned in his world being a virgin was

unusual past a certain age. The age of consent was sixteen, so maybe I was above average when it came to losing my virginity, but really... I didn't think I was ready.

My body certainly wasn't.

Jørgen wasn't.

And Jørgen was the only one I wanted to be so intimate with.

Maybe during one of the holidays when I went back?

CHAPTER 4

I had yet to meet Charlotte's niece and nephew.

That Saturday, Charlotte was having them over and she made tacos, which both Marlene and Kristoffer professed were the best Saturday evening snack food of all time.

I would've helped her out if I hadn't had Nik over, because I didn't mind being in the kitchen. I actually liked it.

Nik and I were in my room, and Nik was studying the easel standing in one corner. I had finished painting the landscape picture two nights before, but I'd left it up there because I was quite happy about it and I liked the scenery.

"This is…" Nik held his finger an inch away from

the canvas. "Ah-hah! Yes, it's the trails up by the graveyard."

I grinned and nodded, happy he'd recognised it. That meant I'd done the landscape justice.

It was a scene from one of the last times Jørgen and I had been on the trail, when the trees and grass were blooming.

I'd poured my heart into that painting to replicate the beauty of spring and the beauty of the landscape I'd had around me all my life.

"You're talented." Nik finally turned towards me. "I can see why you'd study arts. You should continue doing art, not waste away on general studies. It's so boring." He fell down in my chair and leant back, throwing his head back dramatically.

"It'll be worth it," I said. "University, and all that." I was lying on my stomach on my bed, and I propped an elbow on the soft mattress and rested my cheek in my palm.

Nik was wearing loose trousers today, an uncharacteristically normal black. His vest, something he always wore, was the most vulgarly colourful one I'd seen yet. Today it said *I love cocks*.

"So, why exactly are you down here so early? School doesn't start till August."

"Because I've worked my arse off for the past two years for this. I stocked shelves at the supermarket, sat at the till, whatever needed to be done. So now that I'm finally done with work and school and actually have money saved up, I figured I'd head down early and get to know Oslo properly before the hassle of a new school started."

He straightened his head up and turned a wicked grin my way. "I'd also like to check out the nightlife, you know. Like, go out and pull blokes and all that. There so much to choose from here, compared to back home. There's not many gay people back home, especially not many who're out, so pickings are slim. Especially as my best mate's gay and my brother bucks blokes as well when he sees fit. I don't want any of their leftovers. But, like, here I don't even have to worry about that. It's *great*!"

I'd only known Nik for a week, but I already knew we were polar opposites.

He was confident, flamboyant, and out there, not afraid to give of himself. He liked sex—and he wasn't shy about talking about it either. It was refreshing. While I didn't have a sex life, I didn't mind hearing about Nik's rather promiscuous one.

A knock on the door brought our attention away from each other.

Charlotte stuck her head in, glancing between us. "Dinner's ready. Do you want to stay, Nikolai? There's more than enough for us all."

"That would be great, if you don't mind." Nik smiled widely at her and Charlotte smiled back.

"I don't mind at all. Come on down. Martin and Linnea have arrived and we're all ready to start eating." She shut the door after herself.

"You don't get much home cooked food anymore, do you?" I asked as I pushed myself up and out of the bed. "Living at the halls and all."

"I hate cooking," Nik said with passion as he followed me out of my room. "Absolutely hate it. So whenever there's food on offer, of course I say yes." I didn't even have to turn around to know he grinned teasingly.

"Jørgen hates to cook too."

"You know, it's astonishing how much you actually talk about him." Nik hurried up so he could walk by my side down the stairs. He elbowed my side playfully. "You're *so* in love with him."

"I am." There was no point denying it. It was obvious. I thought about Jørgen all the time. I missed him constantly.

"Do you keep in contact, much?" Nik looked at me from out of the corner of his eye.

I shrugged. "Not as much as I'd like us to. I think it's worse for him to talk to me all the time. He's all alone, while I'm… well, I'm not. It's not like I hate it here, it's just that I wish I was back home. Still, this is my home for the next year, and there's nothing I can do about that. I think I'm dealing better than he is."

Nik bit on a fingernail. "You do know," he said hesitantly, "that Jørgen is extremely damaged, right?"

"I do. I've been there through flashbacks and panic attacks. That doesn't mean he can't be loved. Because I do, Nik. I love him so much." I knew it was true. My chest constricted with the simple thought and my stomach jumped. I wished I could tell him, because I hadn't. Not a straight out *I love you*, anyway.

I was young, but I still knew what love was. I still knew I loved him so damn much.

We walked into the dining room side by side.

Charlotte and Marlene were all smiles, like usual.

Kristoffer was engrossed in his phone, so he didn't even look up.

Dad looked over, and his eyes seemed to be drawn directly to Nik's vest. I could see his eyes widen a fraction in surprise, and I had to stifle a laugh. Dad hadn't met Nik before now, so he had no idea just how out there Nik was.

"Dad, this is Nik." Nik had met Charlotte when he'd arrived, so they were already friendly. He shook my Dad's hand, then Marlene's.

My eyes fell on the two people standing next to Kristoffer. They didn't look anything at all like Charlotte and Marlene. It was obvious they were twins, even if they weren't the same gender. They both had thick, straight dark hair and blue eyes. He was a couple of inches taller than her. He wore glasses, and her eyes were heavily made-up.

"This is my nephew, Martin." Charlotte motioned over to them. "And my niece, Linnea."

Nik greeted them cheerfully. He shook Martin's hand and kissed Linnea's cheek. She giggled as she greeted him back. I stepped up next and I found Martin's blue eyes locked on me without blinking.

"Hi," I mumbled, a bit uncomfortable with the attention.

He blushed red the moment I spoke and dropped his head, and I shook my head slightly as I greeted his sister next.

"Nice to meet you," Linnea said, her voice low and melodious.

"Yeah. You too."

I had to admit I wasn't terribly interested in getting to know them. Especially not while Nik was there. I made sure to sit between him and my Dad at our side of the table, because Dad was still eying Nik's shirt with both shock and disdain.

Frankly, it was hilarious.

Charlotte, as usual, sat at the head of the table, with her kids and niece and nephew opposite us. I had Martin opposite me, but he didn't look at me at all anymore.

Great. Someone else who didn't approve of something about me.

I pushed his weird behaviour away and filled my plate. There were shells and tortillas, and my favourite when it came to tacos was definitely the tortilla.

I looked over at Nik while I wrapped my tortilla into a square. He was carefully rolling his into a sausage. He must've felt my eyes on him, because he tilted his head to grin at me.

Charlotte started asking Nik about general stuff, like what he was studying. Marlene came with questions as well, especially when it came to dancing; turned out she was a fan of dance and used to dance herself when she was younger.

Linnea was conversing in low tones with her brother, but they weren't speaking loud enough for me to hear.

After dinner, Nik excused himself as he had to go home.

I followed him to the door.

He pulled on his leather jacket, tied up his pink Converse, then stepped close to me and hugged me. "I had a wicked time today. Actually, I always enjoy spending time with you. I hope you know that."

"Th-thanks." I was surprised at him actually admitting it out loud. I knew he liked me, considering we'd been meeting every day for a week, but actually hearing it... that was nice. "I feel the same, just so you know."

Nik blew me a kiss, then skipped out the door.

I closed it after him with a fond smile, then headed into the kitchen to help with dishes.

Dad was alone in there, and I opened the dishwasher and started putting in the plates he was cleaning under the spring.

"So that's your new friend."

I could tell from Dad's voice that he had more to say.

"What?" I wanted to cut right to the chase. I didn't want him to keep hinting and stalling. If he had something to say about Nik, he could very well come out and say it.

"I hadn't expected him to be quite so..."

"So what?" I asked, a bit harsher than I'd meant to. "So gay? Is that what you mean?"

"Well. Yeah." Dad kept his eyes on the plates he was cleaning, and once they were done he handed them to me without so much as glancing my way.

"You wanted me to have friends, Dad, and now that I do have one you're complaining? And because he looks different from us? Nik's proud of who he is and he isn't afraid to show it."

"That was quite clear, yes. I could read what his vest said. I know exactly what it means—and it's not about animals."

"So what, Dad? He's not your friend, he's mine. Stop judging him. Nik's a really good person and he likes me."

"I just don't want you to be led into…"

"Being led into what?" My voice rose dangerously. "What, Dad? Being led into *what*?"

"That whole scene!" Dad thrust his arms out, splashing water everywhere. "It's very clear what he likes to do with his nights, isn't it?"

"Partying? Have fun? *Sex*?" I asked, staring at him. "Just for your information Dad, I'm old enough to do whatever I want in that department. You don't have anything to say about it. You can't *do* anything about it. What are you going to do if I'm out having sex? Move to another town again? Drag me away from yet another person I've come to care about?"

"Geir!"

"Don't even start. You wanted me to start over here, to get friends. Guess what, Dad? I've got a friend and he's one of the best. I dig Nik. He's fun and exciting and full of life, and he's exactly the kind of friend I've always wanted to have. And you know who I have to thank for it? Jørgen! He gave me Nik's number because he didn't want me to be alone down here. While you didn't really give a shit, did you?"

I slammed the dishwasher closed and strode out of the kitchen. I avoided the dining room, where the others were still seated, and ran up the stairs and into my room.

I couldn't understand why Dad was suddenly complaining. He'd said he'd wanted me to start over here, and I *had*.

Well, I hadn't *completely* started over.

I still missed Jørgen, but I'd done the best I could.

I'd got to know Nik quite well in the past week, and I thought he was a great person. Dad was squeamish because of Nik's way of presenting himself, and that was *not fair*.

Nik was allowed to dress whichever way he wanted, he was allowed to talk whichever way he wanted, and about whatever he wanted. Dad had no right to talk shit about him for that.

He had no right laying into me for it.

He was right about what Nik liked, but that didn't mean I would follow his lifestyle choices. I was old enough to be trusted, and even if he didn't trust me, I was old enough to do whatever I pleased.

I was above the age of consent, so if I had been out pulling, like Nik, Dad couldn't say much about it.

He could forbid it in his home, obviously, but he couldn't control what I did when I was outside of it.

I couldn't help but be angry at him, even if part of me knew he only cared about me.

First he'd been hostile towards Jørgen because he was older than me.

Now he was hostile towards Nik because he didn't dress normally.

What was normal, anyway? Boring, was what it was. Nik was far from boring: he had style, and he had class, and he was simply himself. There should be nothing wrong with that. Nik wasn't lying about who he was. He was honest, and instead of appreciating that, people kept looking down on him and talking bad about him.

I sat down at my desk. My eyes fell on my lined notebook. I'd bought it for school, so it hadn't been used yet. It was just a normal spiraled notebook, I could rip the papers out and leave the last bit of the margin attached to the spiral inside. I flipped it open.

Grabbing a black pilot marker pen from my penholder, I set the tip to paper. I wrote out an entire page before I finally reread.

The page was filled with whinging about my Dad, so I ripped it out and threw it in the rubbish.

Way to sound like a sullen teenager.

I was a bit more objective on the second try, but

that felt wrong too, so I threw that paper in the rubbish as well.

By the third try I felt calmer, more level, and I managed to write a proper letter without raging about my dad. He was mentioned, certainly, but the letter wasn't about him. No matter how angry I was at him, I wasn't about to whinge about it, especially not to Jørgen.

When I'd reached a third down the fourth page, I felt I was done.

I had no idea how to sign it, though.

Best wasn't enough, *best regards* was too formal. Would I dare sign it *love*?

After biting down on my lower lip for a good minute angsting about it, I settled on *yours*.

Because I was.

I was his.

PART II
IT'S BEEN
NINETY-SEVEN DAYS

JØRGEN

CHAPTER 5

The flat was too big, too silent, too much.

I always thought I liked being alone, but I'd learned the past month that I didn't. I didn't like it at all. Being alone *sucked*.

There wasn't anything I could do about it, though.

Geir was gone, and who else did I have?

No one, that was who.

Not a single person.

The doorbell rang.

It startled me, and my skin crawled more than ever. I wanted to scratch myself, but I knew it wouldn't help. It was under my skin. It was my nerves reacting to my anxiety.

I eyed the medication I'd put on the coffee table

earlier. It was prescription, and I'd already taken two earlier, so I couldn't take another one. My psychologist had warned me not to take any more than what the label said.

The doorbell rang again, startling me less now that I knew someone was at my door.

One part of me wanted to get up and open the door, to welcome the company, but the other part was happy to lie on the sofa in my listlessness.

The latter won out.

I wasn't quite sure if I could get up and cross the floor anyway.

The medication was strong and I wasn't used to it. It made me feel weird, dizzy.

I should probably ring my psychologist up about that. Just like I'd told Geir, Daniel had helped me find a woman. I didn't think I could ever relax with another man.

Not that I could relax *ever*, at all, but her being a woman helped.

She couldn't hurt me.

"Jørgen?"

I heard my name being called.

It didn't really matter, though, it was so far away.

My skin might be crawling, but my head was blissfully woozy. It was such a change from the headache I'd had that morning. Seemed two prescription pills and two regular painkillers did wonders.

I didn't know if I should have taken painkillers with the prescription drugs. Probably not, considering I'd taken one prescription pill too many as well.

Still, my head felt blissfully empty, and it was nice. No more being afraid of a flashback or a panic attack.

The sleeping pills I'd been given for proper sleep had actually given me a good night's sleep for once, and mixing them now with antidepressants was giving me a good drowse. Coupled with the painkillers, I was feeling rather calm.

I knew I shouldn't be mixing them, but it made me feel much better.

How bad could it be, right?

"Jørgen?"

A shadow fell over my face, and I slowly shifted my eyes from the ceiling over to whoever was trying to get my attention.

Long blonde hair was what I noticed first, and a heavy fringe stopping right above azure eyes.

I groaned and shifted my eyes back to the ceiling. The ceiling was nice; it was all one colour and it didn't move.

"Jørgen?"

What was she doing here?

Why was she constantly repeating my name?

Couldn't she go away? I had no interest in talking to her. I had no interest in talking to anyone, but least of all her.

"Jørgen? What've you taken?" I could hear her pick up my medication. "Have you mixed all of these? Jørgen?"

I wished she'd go away. I was finally feeling good. I didn't want her to ruin it. I'd had a shitty week and I just wanted one day where I wasn't in therapy, where I didn't have to talk, where I didn't break down from the simplest memory.

One bloody day where everything was kept at a distance.

I wasn't alone anymore, though. Someone else was there. But she wasn't the person I wanted to be there. She was here to talk, and I was done talking. I was so tired of talking.

"I'm calling an ambulance."

My head snapped around. "I'm fine!" My stomach did a sort of flip-flop, and suddenly I wasn't feeling so great as the nausea that had lain dormant while I'd been lying quietly on my back came back full force.

"You're not bloody fine!"

I didn't know what she did, and my body

protested my sudden movements so much I couldn't care less.

When I heard her speak again, I knew she was on the phone.

Possible drug overdose.

I hadn't taken an overdose, I just wanted my fucking head to calm down. I wanted the panic to subside, the panic I *constantly* felt. I was sick and tired of feeling like shit, of feeling like the smallest little thing drew me right back into reliving the past. I didn't want that anymore...

"Jørgen." She was crouched in front of me now, and her hand, firm and warm, stroked over my shoulders. "Come on, shhh. Why're you crying? Jørgen. This is going to be fine. The ambulance will be here and they'll take you to the hospital."

Everything was a blur after that.

I was aware of others crowding me, of being moved.

Christina held on tight to my hand, and I didn't have the energy or will to pull away from her.

Then there were bright lights and several voices talking above me. Someone shone a light in my eyes, and I fought to close them, but the person was insistent. The nausea came back with a vengeance and I vomited.

More voices, but I couldn't hear what they were

saying. I didn't know if I fell asleep, if I fell into unconsciousness, or if they sedated me, but next thing I knew I blinked my eyes open.

A white ceiling stretched out overhead.

It wasn't *my* ceiling.

I blinked several times, making sure I was awake and aware before I dared turn my head.

On my right was a wall with a big window. The blinds were closed so they weren't letting in the sunlight.

I turned my head the other way and caught sight of Daniel sitting quietly in a stool next to the bed, looking at me calmly.

"Hey, Jørgen."

I swallowed, wondering if I could even talk. My throat and mouth felt dry. "Hey," I managed to croak out.

"Do you want to talk about it?"

"No." What was I supposed to say? It was all a blur. "I just wanted one day where I wouldn't break down."

"Mixing medication is not the best way to achieve that."

"I know." Of course I knew. I'd been talking with Daniel ever since Geir left a month ago. Not as my therapist—I didn't know what to think of him as. He wasn't a friend, he wasn't my therapist... but in a sense he was, because I could talk to him about everything and he'd listen. He'd ask me questions, he'd prompt me, just as my psychologist did. "What're you doing here, anyway?"

"We were supposed to meet today and you didn't show up. When I went over to your flat, I met your cousin. She told me you were here. She's worried about you."

My cousin?

I frowned and some images came back to me. Blonde hair, Christina's voice as she talked to me, as she rang for an ambulance. Her hand clutching my arm in the back of the ambulance. Wait… "It's been a day?"

"Yeah." Daniel nodded. "Well, almost. You were brought in yesterday evening, now it's barely noon."

"Why aren't you at work?" *Work… Shouldn't I be at work? No, wait…* I'd been to see my psychiatrist on Friday, which had been the worst session up until then, and then on Saturday I'd wanted to stay in. That's when I'd mixed the pills.

So that made today Sunday.

Daniel raised an eyebrow, but he didn't answer. He could tell I'd already figured it out. He was good like that.

"Can I ask you something, Jørgen?"

"Sure." It wasn't like I could stop him.

"Talking to your cousin, Christina, I got the impression that you do have a family who cares about you. A family who *wants* to care, at least." He stared at me, gauging my reaction. "Why won't you let them? This isn't the family you have issues with, Jørgen. This isn't the family who hurt you and neglected you. This is the other side of your family, and as far as I could understand from Christina, they all worry about you a great deal."

I looked away. I didn't want to think about that.

"What was she doing at my flat?"

"She was getting your mail for you. It's over there. You've got a letter."

I turned my head, and sure enough, there was a small stack on the bedside table. I could see the bright fronts of commercial magazines, and a few white envelopes that could only be bills.

The one on top, however was written out by hand, addressed to me. I recognised that handwriting, and my chest squeezed painfully.

Geir.

I could tell from Daniel's voice that he knew who that letter was from too.

I closed my eyes. What if I'd taken even more pills or if my body had reacted differently to the mix I'd already taken? What if something had happened to me…?

Daniel would've had to tell him. It wasn't long ago he'd lost his beloved dog. What had I been doing? Trying to make him lose the other person he'd come to care about?

"Don't beat yourself up, Jørgen," Daniel said quietly. "No lasting damage has been done. I think you've learned to not mix medication again. Though you'll have to talk to the doctors about it. It's for them to determine."

I didn't want to think about my impending chat with some doctor—all I could think about was Geir, and that letter.

I opened my eyes and slowly turned my head to look at Daniel. "Do you think he'll come back?"

Daniel stared at me, serious as ever, and my stomach knotted. "He says he will. I know he cares for you a lot."

My eyes burned as the tears started falling.

I missed him so much. I couldn't even describe just how much I missed him. He'd been just a kid I'd kept from freezing to death, but he'd become so much more. How could he possibly have buried himself so permanently under my skin in only a few months?

Crying in front of Daniel wasn't an issue for me. I'd done it before. It came with the territory, didn't it? He was a psychiatrist and used to seeing people cry.

TT KOVE

But when Christina suddenly walked into my room, I was quick to try and wipe the tears away. It didn't help, they kept on coming, and she'd seen what I'd done anyway.

"Jørgen." She looked alarmed and threw a glance over at Daniel. I didn't know if they had some sort of silent communication going on, but she did step further into the room and turn her focus back on me. "I was so worried about you. I'm glad you're fine." She twisted her hands together, kind of like Geir did whenever he was nervous.

I didn't know what to say to that, so instead I turned to Daniel. "When can I go home?"

"That depends."

"On what?"

"You just took an overdose on prescription medication. They're not going to release you just like that. They'll be in here to talk to you, to determine your state of mind. They might release you if they find there's little chance of this happening again, but they won't if you go home alone, I can promise you that."

My stomach knotted in dread.

Christina glanced between us.

"No," I said. "I am *not* staying with you and Jo. No way." I couldn't face Jo. I was already raw, meeting him now would beat me down further. It wouldn't be of any help.

"I was thinking more about your uncle," Daniel shot in. "I spoke with him earlier. He's a doctor. He works here. He knows what to do."

"Please, Jørgen," Christina said, almost begging. "It's only him, Maria, Ben, and Alex there now, after I moved out and Andreas went to the army."

I was surprised at that last part. "Andreas' in the army?"

She nodded. "He left at the beginning of the month for the obligatory twelve months."

I hadn't spoken to Andreas since Christmas, and then it had only been a few words.

So Andreas was gone.

That left Ben. I had a hard time stomaching Ben because he was so very different from me. He was out there, not afraid to speak his mind or be who he was.

Alex… the name rang a bell, but I had no idea who it was. I couldn't be arsed to ask either.

"They won't discharge you unless you stay with him," Daniel said. "If you don't want to, they'll put you on suicide watch."

"I wasn't trying to—"

"Doesn't matter what you'd tried to do or not, Jørgen. That's what it looked like."

I closed my eyes. The tears had dried, but my face felt blotched and my eyes dry, like the tears had taken all moisture with them.

"I've spoken to Gina," Daniel continued. "Told her what happened. She's writing you up a sick leave from work, and you'll have sessions with her every other day for the foreseeable future."

I couldn't argue with that. The sessions with her drained me, and work suffered for it. I'd gone from zero sick days to several in the past month because some days I couldn't even dredge up the will to get out of bed.

My mind was completely exhausted after every session. My body too, from experiencing flashbacks and panic attacks, sometimes one or the other, sometimes both.

I was drowning in my memories, and I didn't know how to reach the surface.

CHAPTER 6

I went home with Thomas, my dad's youngest brother, after his shift was over that evening.

Thomas was a doctor, but he hadn't been the one to receive me in the A&E the evening before.

I supposed that was good, considering everything.

I didn't have any of my pills. Daniel had taken all of them: the sleeping pills, the antidepressants, and the painkillers. I reckoned he was giving them back to Gina, so she could evaluate the chosen prescriptions again. I didn't know if I'd get them back or if she would start me on other pills.

One thing was for certain, and that was that I

would get *something*. I couldn't function without the pills lately; everything was too hard.

"Christina's making dinner," Thomas said as he parked his car in the driveway.

I hoisted my bag out of the backseat and followed him up to the front door. We'd stopped by my flat so I could get a change of clothes and toiletries. I hoped I wouldn't have to stay for long. I wanted to go back to my own flat again—I already missed it.

I hadn't been to Thomas' house since Christmas. And I'd left pretty quickly then too. There'd been too many people. I hadn't been able to deal with it.

I couldn't really deal with much, could I?

Staying there seemed like a nightmare, and now that my sleeping pills had been confiscated, I wouldn't be able to sleep either. Strange beds were the worst thing that could ever happen to me. I struggled falling asleep in my own bed. Certainly struggled to actually *stay* asleep.

I could feel Thomas' eyes on me, but I kept my head down and toed out of my shoes.

He headed for the kitchen, and I followed.

My anxiety ratcheted up every step I took towards that door.

Some, if not all, of the house's residents would be in there. I wondered if they knew, if Christina had told them.

I hoped she hadn't, but then again... how else would I explain my presence? It wasn't like *I* was ever going to admit to it. Accidentally overdosing on medication... I felt like a complete failure.

"Dinner's ready," Christina said the moment I stepped over the threshold. She turned from the stove with a stock pot and put it down in the middle of the table, which was set for six.

Thomas sat down at the head of the table, and Christina took the available spot on his side, next to her sister Maria.

I took the last place, which was opposite Maria and next to a bloke with unruly black hair. I remembered him from Christmas.

He was Andreas' boyfriend, of course. He smiled slightly at me but didn't say anything. I was grateful; I didn't want to talk.

Ben kept shooting glances my way, but for once in his life he managed to restrain himself from speaking his mind. Ben was... well, an emo or a goth. I wasn't that into teen slang, but he dressed all in tight black clothes, and his black hair was long and straight and fell over his eyes. He also wore a ton of eyeliner.

Maria, my youngest cousin, was Christina's little sister and looked as such. Blonde hair, blue eyes, same facial shape. She hardly ever wore make-up, though, and she wore glasses and usually had her nose buried in a book.

I didn't mind Maria, as she hardly ever said much. It was the loud family members I couldn't stand to be around, like Ben.

Dinner was a rather quiet affair.

It was probably because of me.

Either they knew what had happened or they were confused about my presence. I didn't know which one was worse.

I managed to get some food in me, but my stomach cramped and I didn't finish the entire plate.

Christina blocked my path when everyone else went to clean their plates and put them in the dishwasher.

"I did up my old room for you," she said in a low voice so no one else could hear.

So she *hadn't* told on me.

I felt grateful towards her for that. I'd never felt that way towards her before.

"Bring your bag, I'll show you."

Yeah, she'd have to. I'd never been in her room before. I'd never been in any of their rooms. The living room, kitchen, and backyard were the only places I'd ever spent any amount of time in at Thomas' house.

Christina's room was pretty bare, which I

suspected had not always been the case. She was living with Jo, so she must've taken most of her stuff with her. All the furniture was there, the usual like a bed, a desk, a closet, and a chest of drawers.

I put my bag down on the bed, which she'd made for me.

When I turned back around, she stood right inside the door.

"Why don't you come over one day, Jørgen?" she asked lightly. "You haven't seen our flat. We'd really like it if you'd come over for a visit."

I shook my head long before she'd even finished her sentence.

"Why not?" She was becoming frustrated. I could tell from the slight rise in her voice. "Jo loves you, you know that, right?"

I shook my head again. "Stop it."

"I can't stop it. You obviously need to hear it. He's your brother; you should be leaning on him, not pushing him away."

Now I was the one who got frustrated. "What has Jo ever done for me? The answer's very simple. He's done *nothing*." Not a fucking thing. I couldn't just forgive and forget everything. Twenty-two years of him not giving a shit about me was not something I could work through.

Christina pressed her lips together. "He has his

reasons, you know. Maybe you should hear them before you make up your mind about him." With that said, she turned and stalked out of the room.

I went over to shut the door, then walked back over to fall down on the bed. How could Jo possibly have *reasons* for anything? I was the one who'd been beaten, locked up, molested...

What had he ever experienced?

He'd never been in my situation, he'd kept away from it all, while I'd been the one who'd had to take all the anger, who'd had to take all of my uncle's advances.

Jo didn't have *reasons*.

None that would hold up against everything *I'd* been through.

My mobile vibrated, and I turned around on my back so I could fish it out of my pocket.

It was Tarjei.

"Hi," I said into the receiver.

"Where are you?" Tarjei asked, his voice chipper. "I've been ringing your doorbell for *forever*."

"I'm over at Thomas' house." Seemed Christina hadn't even told Tarjei, because if he'd known he certainly wouldn't be feeling so chipper. He'd be frantic and worried if he knew.

"What on earth are you doing over there? You

suddenly felt like a bit of family time?" His voice was teasing now, but still light.

"I'm just… just staying here for a few days."

He got quiet in the other end. "Are you all right?"

"Yeah." That was a lie. I wasn't all right, not really.

I was miserable. I was drowning in my own misery. I was all alone with it too, because Tarjei tried his best to be there for me, but he didn't really understand what it was like to have to live with everything I'd been through.

"You sure?"

"Yeah." I wasn't. Not at all.

Tarjei was silent again for a while. "Ring me up if you need anything. Anything at all, okay? Whenever. I don't mind."

It was nice to know he cared. I knew he did, but the confirmation was good once in a while. I didn't think I ever would ring him, however, and I thought he knew that.

Still, he offered.

"I will."

We hung up, and I let my hand drop to the bed with a sigh.

I hadn't told him I was on a sick leave from work from now on. That would only make him worry more and I didn't want that.

He'd find out tomorrow.

Maybe I'd feel up to actually talking to him then.

Because I sure wasn't now. I was tired, and ashamed. I was without medication for the first time in a month, and I was quickly realising that it had been a help. A crutch.

Why hadn't I been happy with it? Why had I taken more than what was prescribed?

I closed my eyes. I wished Geir was here. Maybe things wouldn't feel so dreary if he'd been here with me.

He'd made things better for those five months we'd known each other.

I wanted him back.

I sat up straight and dragged my bag onto my lap.

He'd sent me a letter.

How could I have forgotten about that?

I drew the white envelope out of the side pocket of my bag, then laid back down.

My heart beat in my chest as I looked at his neat, elegant handwriting. It was so different from mine, which was almost unintelligible.

Why had he sent me a letter?

My heart beat quicker.

It could just be a regular letter, but... it could also be bad news. Did I want to open it if it contained bad news?

What if he was calling it quits?

What if he wasn't coming back? Not for autumn holiday, not next year, not ever.

Could I take it if it was that?

"He'll come back." Daniel had been so sure that he would. He knew his nephew better than I did. He should, anyway. In certain aspects, perhaps, but in some I was certain *I* was the one who knew Geir better.

I ripped the envelope open and took the letter out. There were four handwritten pages, folded double.

I unfolded them and started to read.

Jørgen,

> *I miss you!*
>
> *I've been trying to write this letter three times and I always start with those three words. They're true, so very true.*
>
> *Are you doing all right? I know you aren't telling me everything when we speak on the phone, and that's okay, because I know you don't like to talk about things. I hope you are though. All right, that is.*
>
> *I'm doing fine, I guess.*
>
> *Nik's awesome, so thank you for giving me his number. I already consider him a friend and he considers*

me one as well. I like spending time with him. He's fun, he's open and he's honest. He wears the most outrageous vests, but they're part of him, aren't they? I like them.

Dad doesn't, he thinks they're too vulgar. He thinks Nik will lead me astray. That I will take after him when it comes to partying and sex. Like that's going to happen.

Even if Nik and I are totally different, though, we fit so nicely together. It's easy being around him. I think we can become great friends, and I've got you to thank for that!

I know I've already told you this, but I can't help liking it here a little bit. The house is big, with more than enough space for all of us, but at the same time it's homey, you know?

I already love Charlotte, she's an amazing woman.

Her daughter, Marlene, is awesome too. I haven't really got to know Kristoffer, the son, much. He sticks to himself when he's home, which isn't often at all. He's always out with mates.

I met Charlotte's niece and nephew today. They seemed nice enough, though the nephew hardly ever looked at me all night. I guess he doesn't like me, but what else is new, right? Still, I've got Nik, so I'm happy. That's all I wanted, after all: one friend. Thanks to you, I've finally got one. Besides you, that is.

So yeah, I miss you.

I asked Dad if I could come home for a week or two before school started. Nik's driving home, so I could've gone with him. Dad didn't think it was a good idea though. It sucks, but what can I do? At least he hasn't protested about the Autumn holiday, so I will come visit you then.

He can't stop me then, I swear.

Dad also wants me to get another dog. Can you believe it? I don't want another dog. It would feel too much like replacing Charo and I can't even stand the thought of it. Dad doesn't understand, and we had an argument about it. Like we do about anything lately.

I've never argued with Dad before in my life, and now it seems like we're making up for all that time. We make up again, of course, but sometimes he makes a comment or a decision I don't agree with, and I can't help but be furious with him. Like with Nik, or about me coming home to visit this summer.

He can stop me from coming home now, but he can't stop me from seeing Nik. I guess I should be grateful for what I have. And there's the autumn holiday. It's only a week, but at least I'll get to see you again. I'm counting down the days. I miss you so much!

Yours,
Geir

I wiped my eyes as I finished the letter, relieved that there was no bad news, that he didn't want to break things off between us. He could've come back in the summer, but as long as he was coming home for the next holiday I was happy.

As long as I knew I would actually get to see him again, it would all be fine.

If only I could get my own psyche in order.

I was seeing Gina first thing in the morning. I hadn't spoken to her myself, Daniel had taken care of it for me, but she'd come in earlier to have a chat with me before the rest of her patients. I felt bad about her coming in early, but for once I actually felt a need to see her, so I wasn't about to complain—I wanted to feel better, although so far therapy only seemed to make everything worse.

I read over the letter a second time. I knew most of it from talking to him on the phone, but the fact that he was arguing a lot with his dad was news to me.

As was the fact that Yngvar wanted him to get another dog.

I wished he could've come back during the summer, but maybe it was for the best that he didn't, as I needed to sort myself out.

Needed to come to terms with my past.

I wasn't any good company for the moment. With

the draining sessions where I actually *had* to talk about it all, plus trying out new medication… I wasn't fit to have company. I would most likely be prescribed new medication after my session tomorrow, which would screw with both my head and my body again, like the first ones had done.

Gina said I would get used to it, my body just needed some time to work out the kinks.

I wondered how long it would take to find the right medication and just how long it would take for my body to work itself out.

CHAPTER 7

I couldn't sleep.

The bed was unfamiliar, the room was unfamiliar, and the sounds were unfamiliar. I lay tossing and turning, and couldn't for the life of me find a comfortable position.

My brain was working double, noticing how everything was unlike my own flat to trying to figure out what all the sounds could mean. I was used to the sounds in my flat, but not these ones.

I knew they weren't anything sinister, just the normal sounds that came with a house. The house wasn't new either, and there would always be some sounds, but I couldn't relax.

I gave up eventually and got up from the bed. When I opened my door, only silence greeted me. All lights were off. I checked the clock and saw that it was past one in the morning.

Everyone was asleep.

I wasn't even sure where everyone's rooms were, so I walked slowly and carefully down the hallway and to the first floor.

All the lights were off downstairs too, but it was July, which meant that it was never truly dark outside. More like dusk, or perhaps twilight.

Still, it was enough for me to see where I was going. I headed for the kitchen, wanting a glass of water.

I nearly had a heart attack when I walked right into someone as I turned into the kitchen.

Something wet splashed down the front of my jumper.

"Oh god, I'm so sorry!"

I looked up from my own chest and caught sight of Alex's dark hair and wide eyes. He clutched a glass to his chest, and his T-shirt was wet too.

"It's okay." My heart still beat triple, but I took several deep breaths to calm myself down.

His eyes were wide and focused on me. He tilted his head slightly, and I could see then as the light from the window shone on him that his face was wet. Judging from the red eyes, it wasn't water splashed on his face.

"Are you all right?" I now felt extremely awkward. How was I supposed to deal with someone who was crying? When it was Geir, it was okay, because I could just wrap my arms around him and he'd take comfort in that, but Alex… I didn't know Alex. I'd only met him once, at Christmas, and that was seven months ago. I wasn't sure I'd even spoken to him then.

"No," he answered, then he seemed to realise what he'd said and he shook his head. "I mean, yeah. I'm okay."

"Doesn't look like it. Do you want to talk about it?"

He got a guarded look on his face. "You'd be interested in talking to me?"

"Sure." I shrugged. Why not? I had nothing better to do. My mind was on overdrive and hearing his troubles would sure be better than constantly thinking about my own. "You don't have to, if you'd rather go back to sleep." I stepped around him to get my own glass of water.

"I can't sleep."

I glanced back at him. "Me neither."

We looked at each other silently for a long moment.

"Want to go in the living room?" he asked. "Sofa's much more comfortable than the kitchen chairs."

I nodded, grabbed my glass, and followed him across the hall. The living room was even lighter, because there were almost floor-to-ceiling double glass doors leading out into the backyard.

I could see him dry his face and eyes out of the corner of my eye. I sat down on the other end of the sofa from where he was sitting, and after taking a long gulp of water, I set the glass on the coffee table in front of me.

"It's silly, really," Alex said after a couple of minute's silence. "I mean… he's only gone for a year. And he's got twenty days off-time, so it's not like I won't see him during that year."

"You miss Andreas?"

"Yeah. It's silly to cry over something like that, I know."

"It's not." I stared out into the darkened back-yard. "It's not silly at all."

"Do you have someone you miss?" Alex asked tentatively.

"Yeah." I glanced at him and could see he was curious. "My boyfriend. He's only seventeen, so when his dad wanted to move to Oslo, he had to go with him."

"Oh. That… sucks." He clenched and unclenched his fists, and the movement drew my attention. He was only wearing a T-shirt, and it was light enough for me to see his skin. His scarred skin.

I darted my eyes up to look at him again, and his slowly rose from his arms as well. He'd seen what I'd looked at, and I could tell he was embarrassed by the flush creeping up his neck.

He turned his arms over, hiding the underside of them.

"You don't have to be embarrassed." I ran one thumb over my own forearm, where I had my own thick vertical scar. I never gave those scars much thought, because those were scars I'd inflicted on myself. I had no problems going around in a tee or a vest, because I didn't much care what people thought of them—but I didn't flash them at people either.

"They're ugly," he muttered. "No one was supposed to be awake, so I went up in short sleeves."

"Does Andreas think they're ugly?"

He snorted. "Of course he does. He's just too nice to actually say it." He ran a hand across his face then and sighed. "I'm sorry. That sounded very bitter. I'm just in a really bad phase right now. My medication usually helps, but sometimes... sometimes not even that can stop it."

"It?"

He glanced at me. "The depression. Sometimes I go into these really dark moods. They've lessened ever since I got together with Andreas, but they haven't gone away entirely. Not yet. They might. Or not." He looked at me again. "I'm sorry. You didn't ask to know any of that."

"I don't mind. You're not alone. At least you don't take too much of your medication and end up having to be babysat."

His eyes were on me again, I could feel it. "Did— did that happen to you? Is that why you're here?"

I nodded. I stroked my thumb over my scar again, but on the other arm this time. I rolled up my sleeve on both arms and turned them around to show Alex.

His eyes widened as he looked down at the thick white scars going from the crook of my elbow all the way down to my wrists.

"I did my research on how best to cut to die quickly," I muttered. "Horizontal cutting doesn't really do much, but cutting vertically, along the main artery—now *that* bleeds."

He wet his lips. "How did—I mean… How did you survive that?"

"My friend, Tarjei. He found me. Called 1-1-3. I woke up in the hospital. I was put on suicide watch."

I hadn't talked, but Jo had gone to the police after that. My uncle was taken in for questioning, was released, shot his brains out… then my parents had been taken in for questioning.

84

They were prosecuted. My uncle would've been as well, but he'd been too much of a coward to face everything he'd done.

"I don't cut to kill myself."

"I know." A brief smile flitted over my lips. "You cut horizontally. If you'd really wanted to die, you would've done it vertically. And you would've done it properly the one time you *did* do it."

He ran his left fingers over the scars covering his right forearm. "I planned on killing myself," he said. "I had no one. No one cared. I cleaned out my locker so no one else would have to do it and I carried all my books home with me. Some tosser knocked them out of my hands so they scattered on the ground. That cemented my decision further, but then—" His breath caught in his throat. "Then Andreas was there. He's been there ever since. I appreciate him, and his mere presence, more than words can express. Which is why it's so hard now here without him."

He started to cry again, but he simply let the tears fall. "He's been there ever since that third week of school. He was there for me when I was bashed… he's been there for me for almost a year. He's my rock and now he's gone."

"Bashed?" I asked, numbly.

His eyes brimmed with tears. "I was bashed last November. An iron bar, straight to the head." He touched a point on his head, and now that my attention was brought to it I could see that his hair was shorter around that point.

Shit. "Why?"

"Didn't like me being gay. Especially not *gaying up* Andreas."

"Isn't Andreas gay?" I had no idea about any of my family's sexualities. I knew Christina's, since she was dating Jo, and Ben's, since he was so bloody obvious, but other than that… I didn't know my own family at all.

"Gay for me." Alex grinned slightly. It was probably an inside joke, because I sure didn't get what there was to smile about. "He's bisexual. He only came out when we got together though, and, well, *some people* didn't like it."

"Was there any lasting damage after the bashing?"

He shook his head. "I was lucky. The doctors said that if it had hit even a fraction to the side, I could've died. Or at least ended up a vegetable."

That was horrible. I hadn't heard about that incident at all. Perhaps I should start reading the paper. Or keep in contact with my family. It must've been a horrible deal for everyone involved.

I'd never experienced homophobia, not like that.

Every bad thing I'd experienced was at the hand of either my mum or my uncle.

"Why are you staying here when Andreas is gone?"

"My parents are shit, and I don't like them being at each other's throats all the time. They drove my siblings away, and now they've driven me away. It's the story of their lives."

"I'm sorry," I offered lamely. I didn't know what else to say.

"Don't be. They've made their choice." He pursed his lips. "Thomas is awesome. He let me stay here, first with Andreas, and now he's even letting me stay now that Andreas' in the army. He's more a father to me than my own has been all my life."

"He tends to do that, Thomas."

He'd taken care of Ben since Ben was a kid, then he'd taken Christina, Andreas, and Maria in when their dad had offed himself.

Thomas was the only normal one of the siblings. My dad was the oldest, and he didn't give a shit about anything but himself. The middle brother, Andreas' dad, hanged himself in their garage. Hanna, the only girl in the generation, was dead. I didn't know what her deal had been.

Thomas… Thomas had taken care of their children when they hadn't been able to themselves.

Besides me and Jo, because what had been going on in our family had been kept secret for too long for anyone to do anything about it.

It all made me wonder though what kind of childhood *they'd* had. I knew my mum and uncle's childhood must've been bad. How else could they have turned into the monsters they'd been? The monster my mum still was, only she too was locked up in mental facility.

But my dad's side of the family... Something couldn't have been right. My granddad had been dead a long time, and grandma didn't even live in the country anymore.

Everyone was damaged.

I wondered what it would be like to not be plagued by my traumatic past. I wondered if there even existed someone who hadn't experienced something traumatic. It seemed unlikely.

Everyone had their personal demons.

Every family had skeletons in their closet.

"Yeah," Alex sighed, bringing me out of my deep thoughts. "He's wonderful. They're all wonderful."

I glanced sideways at him, saw the small smile playing on his lips.

Maybe he's right. Maybe they all were *wonderful*. Maybe I should give them all a chance.

Except I couldn't give Jo a chance. If Jo came around, I was our of there.

I needed more therapy, I needed more medication, before I could face my brother head on.

"Thanks for talking to me. You didn't have to." He glanced up at me, almost shyly.

I turned my head to stare out the big windows, unable to meet his gaze. "I don't mind."

"Maybe we should hang out sometime?" It came out quickly, in a rush of breath, as if he wanted to get to get the words out there before he chickened out.

It reminded me of Geir. Of that time he'd shown up at my door and asked if I wanted to go to the cinema with him. That time he'd told me all he wanted was a friend…

All I wanted was a friend too. Since Geir was gone, I was down one friend and one boyfriend. I had Tarjei, but we were so different. Alex on the other hand… he was more like me.

"Yeah."

Geir had opened himself up to Nik—and gained a friend out of it. I should do the same. Being lonely sucked—but at least now we could be lonely together.

He missed his boyfriend too, after all.

CHAPTER 8

I watched as Gina's pencil tapped against the top paper of her notebook. It was easier to watch that than to look her in the eyes.

I didn't know what to say or how to even begin to sort my thoughts out.

"Do you want to tell me what happened?" Gina prodded eventually. I wasn't sure how long I'd been sitting in silence, staring at her pencil, but it must've been a while.

Usually she let me be if I needed time to sort my thoughts.

"I took too many pills."

"*Why* did you take too many?"

I shrugged, then leant back and lifted my gaze to the ceiling. "It was too much. I needed—" I didn't even know what I needed. I had no clue. "I needed to *not* feel for a bit."

"And do you think taking too many pills was the right way to do it?" I could still hear her pencil tapping on the paper.

"No." I didn't even have to think about the answer to that. It was a no-brainer. "It was definitely the wrong way to do it. But they were there—it was so easy to just take more."

Maybe I had done it deliberately.

Maybe I had wanted—no.

I wanted to forget, to get better, but I didn't want to *die*. Not now when I had something to live for.

She was silent for a while.

My thoughts rolled around in circles.

Her pencil scratched on paper now, not tapping, and I realised she was writing.

I finally turned my gaze on her—the first time since I'd entered her office. "I'm guessing I won't be leaving here with a prescription for those pills again."

She smiled, but it was tight. "No, Jørgen, you will not. We'll try new ones, see if those'll fit you better." She wrote down something else. "What were you thinking about before you took the extra pills? What was your mood like?"

"I couldn't stop thinking. About my uncle. About Geir. That I don't like to be alone anymore."

"How did that realisation make you feel?"

"Lonely."

I was lonely without Geir.

He hadn't even been gone two months and I'd already been reduced to a wreck who had—accidentally or deliberately, I wasn't even sure myself—OD'ed on my own medication. Medication that was supposed to make me feel better, but made me feel even more like shit than usual.

"You have family, Jørgen. You're staying with your uncle now. Is that lonely?"

"It's too much. Too many people." Even without Christina and Andreas living there, the house felt filled up.

"Do they bother you?"

"Not really, no." I'd kept to myself, except dinner the evening before. And my chat with Alex, but I'd initiated that one, and Alex hadn't been so bad. "I met someone new and he's all right."

Her eyebrows inched up questioningly. "At your uncle's house?"

"My cousin's boyfriend. We're a bit alike." My left hand ran over my right forearm, over the underside of it, where my scars were.

"He lives with your uncle?" She asked, trying to

wrap her head around the intricate living arrangements.

I nodded. "He does. My cousin's in the army, but he's got his room."

"I see." Some more writing on her pad. "And you feel a connection to him?"

"I guess."

She met my gaze. "Do you feel you could be friends?"

"Yeah." Absolutely. That was one thing I *was* certain of.

"What about Tarjei?"

"What about him?"

"He's your friend."

"Yeah…?" I wasn't sure what she was getting at.

"How is your friendship going?" She cocked her head to one side, and her long brown ponytail slid over her shoulder to rest against the front of her blouse.

"Like it always has been." Close friends, but with a certain distance. "We don't have much in common, but we see each other. If not in our spare time, then every day at work."

"But you're not working now. Do you spend time together now then?"

I shrugged again. "Sometimes."

"Do you feel disconnected from him?"

"No." Of course not. Tarjei was my best friend. Nothing could change that. "Tarjei's been there through everything. He knows me better than anyone."

"Even better than Geir?"

And we're back on that subject.

It was the hardest subject to cover, besides my past.

"Yeah." That hurt to acknowledge, because I wanted Geir to be the person closest to me, but it was the truth. "Geir doesn't know much about my past. I've mentioned some things, and I suppose he's guessed at others, but he doesn't know everything."

"Is there anyone who *does* know everything?" Her gaze was intense now.

"Not everything, no." There were certain things not even Tarjei knew about.

Pencil scratched on paper. "Not even me?"

I couldn't face her anymore, so I turned my head away. "No."

She was silent for a while.

I eventually flicked my gaze over her to see her gazing down at her notes. She wrote something down quickly, then lifted her head again. She seemed determined—and my stomach lurched in dread.

"I think it's time we get to those things, Jørgen."

Maybe she was right. Maybe I'd been wrong not

telling her everything before. But my childhood was like a horror film—and just like that particular genre, it wasn't anything I wanted to experience. Especially not over again, even if it was just inside my mind.

"Yeah."

I didn't relish it. Not at all.

I *dreaded* it.

But I was in this to get better.

If Geir came back, I wanted to be a functional human being instead of the mess I was now.

He deserved that.

And, in the end, I guess I deserved it to.

I WAS TOO antsy to stay inside. No one was home, not that I knew, but it felt too stifling. I had to get out, do something, get some fresh air.

Alex was in the driveway when I opened the door —and he was grabbed and kissed by some other bloke.

He pushed at the bloke's chest, almost frantic, and took a step back from him. "You shouldn't have done that," I heard him mumble as he wiped at his lips.

I felt faintly embarrassed to witness this and debating going back inside. But when Alex looked up at me and our gazes met, I simply stood there all awkward.

"Fuck this shit," the bloke who'd kissed him snapped, then shouldered his way past Alex, who stumbled to the side.

"Glenn!" Alex yelled after him, turning on the spot.

The bloke didn't stop.

I walked down the stairs, ready to get away from the drama.

"Where are you going?" Alex turned back to me.

I shrugged. "Out for a walk? Want to join me?"

"Yeah. Okay."

We headed down the road in silence.

"You can ask if you want," he said eventually, hands buried deep in his pockets and his shoulders hunched.

"It's none of my business." The bloke hadn't been Andreas, who was Alex boyfriend, but Alex clearly hadn't been a willing participant in that kiss. So I didn't see any sort of problem with the situation. If Alex *had* kissed him back, now that would've been something else entirely.

Not that it would be my business then either.

"He kissed me. He's struggling." He bit his lower lip, hands coming up to rub at his neck. "Please, just, don't tell anyone about what you saw."

"Who am I going to tell?" I had no one in my life I was comfortable enough to gossip with, even if I had wanted to go slandering about it.

"I don't know." He buried his hands in his pockets again.

Silence descended on us again as he walked deep in thoughts.

I didn't mind. I liked silence. Especially silence that wasn't uncomfortable.

"Have you always known you're gay?"

I blinked, startled by his question. "I guess. I never really thought about it before."

"Before?"

"Before I met Geir."

Before Geir, my life had been all about avoiding triggers. About not thinking about my childhood and everything my uncle had done to me. How my own mum had neglected and abused me.

"Oh, right. Do you talk to him often?"

"Every couple of days." Not that we had much to say to each other. He was usually the one who kept the conversation going. "He wrote me a letter."

"That's nice." He smiled.

"Yeah." It was. I still wasn't sure *why* he'd written one though, when he could've just as easily told me all the letter entailed over the phone. "Geir makes everything more bearable." I didn't know where that came from, it simply left my mouth without my brain filtering it. "When he left, it was like—like nothing really mattered anymore. Being with him made everything hurt just a little less."

"I know that feeling," he agreed with a small nod.

My phone chimed in my pocket, disturbing the silence, startling me. Once I placket it out of my pocket to look at the screen, I shut it off.

Alex eyed me.

"It was just a friend. Tarjei."

"Aren't you going to answer him?"

I shook my head. "I'm not up to talking at the moment." Tarjei would be all cheerful, like he always was with me. I couldn't take that now, not after the session I'd had earlier with Gina. After everything I'd told her.

We walked in silence for a long time after all. Silence all the way to the graveyard, and through the upper par of the cemetery, as well as the beginning of the trail.

I tried not to look down through the trees at the graveyard itself. Kay was down there, my uncle, Geir's mum… I had no need to see the first two graves, but the third one… Maybe I should visit her.

Now that Geir or Yngvar wasn't here anymore, I reckoned she didn't get many visitors. I'd never known her, she'd died when Geir was only seven, but she was his mum. She meant a lot to him. And as he meant a lot to me, perhaps I should make sure her grave was well tended until he came back home.

Someone came running around the outcrop in front of us, almost crashing right into Alex.

"Wow!" Maria managed to stop herself right before she ran headfirst into Alex, and he put his hands on her shoulder to steady her. "Alex. I didn't see you there. Damn. You scared me half to death." She bent over, put her hands on her knees, and gathered her breath.

"I'm sorry," Alex said, though why he should be sorry for anything was beyond me. She was the one who'd come running at us.

"It's okay." She straightened up to smile at him. Then she seemed to realise I was there. "Jørgen." She regarded me curiously for a few seconds before she put her headphones back on and set off at a run again.

"What was that look for?"

I shrugged. "I guess she wonders why I'm staying with you." I got those looks from not only her, but from Ben as well.

Something caught my attention up ahead.

It was a red bench.

The red bench.

I gazed at it, transfixed, until we were past it and I couldn't anymore.

"Third time I met Geir, he was sitting on that bench. With his dog." I didn't know where that confession came from. Why was I telling Alex? I didn't actually know him. "I guess that's when everything started for real."

Alex glanced over his shoulder to look at said bench.

I stared down at the ground, at the pebbles crunching under my shoes as I walked.

He didn't say anything, and I didn't either.

What was there to say, after all?

CHAPTER 9

*A*fter a week of therapy every other day and a new set of medications that worked a lot better than the previous ones, I was finally given the all-clear to go home.

I couldn't have been happier; it was taxing staying with Thomas. There were always people around, and I didn't deal so well with people.

Alex, however, became a permanent fixture in my life after my time over there. I didn't really have anyone else, and neither did he. We had things in common, so we could talk together without it becoming awkward. We could also be quiet together without any awkwardness, and that was nice.

It was quite obvious that he needed someone to

talk to, now that his boyfriend, and previous confi-
dante, was gone for the next year.

I also, to my astonishment, found myself telling
Alex about certain things I so far only had told Gina.
Stuff about my life I hadn't even told Geir.

Geir kept sending me letters.

I appreciated them more than I could ever say, but
I never once replied.

He never mentioned it when we talked on the
phone, so I hoped he didn't mind. Writing a letter
wasn't my forte. He did that too wonderfully for me
to even attempt it—he was artistic where I was
practical.

Things calmed down with my new medication.

I wasn't feeling as raw anymore, like I would
break at every turn I made.

The sessions with Gina progressed to three times
a week, then twice as the months passed.

The sessions with her were always hard, but I
liked to think that I'd started to process what had
happened to me. I liked to think it wasn't all thanks
to the medication.

It didn't mean I was any less lonely.

I still wished Geir would come back. I'd become
so used to him, and I'd actually been able to sleep
with him in my bed the last few times he'd stayed the
night. It was nice that I didn't wake up from every

single sound anymore when he was there. That I could relax in his company, in his presence at night.

After hearing Alex's story, especially about the bashing, I'd promised myself to start paying more attention to what went on in our town.

To achieve that, I'd decided to start a subscription of the paper. I was currently browsing through it, seeing nothing of interest. They didn't have much to write about.

What a dull small town we lived in.

I was about to skip over yet another page when a small picture next to an ad caught my attention.

Our Golden Retriever pup

We regret that, due to us both having full work schedules, we don't have time for our Golden Retriever pup anymore. We would like to see him go to a nice home, where he will be well cared for. He is eight months old. Housebroken, knows to walk on a leash, needs lots of love. E-mail for more information.

I stared at the e-mail address, then up at the picture of the dog again.

A dog...

Charo had been such a good and loving companion to Geir through eleven years.

Getting a dog for myself hadn't been something I'd ever thought about or wanted before, but it struck now and it struck *hard*.

I had a lot to offer a dog: I owned my own flat, I had a steady job, I liked to go on hikes, I had nothing but spare time on my hands when I wasn't working.

Now I was only working half the time, because of my sick leave.

I'd all but begged Gina to lift the sick leave.

I needed something to do, and work was the only thing I could do. She'd recommended I still be fifty percent on sick leave, and I'd taken it. As long as I could work a little bit, I'd been happy.

Dragging my laptop over, I powered it up. Then I quickly wrote out an e-mail before I could second-guess myself.

As I hit send, my doorbell rang.

I didn't even manage to get up off the sofa before Tarjei came into my flat.

"Hey, mate." He carried a plastic bag on one hand. I eyed it curiously as he came over to the coffee table. "I've got crisps, beer, and an action flick." He took each item out of the bag as he spoke. "This is new, so I reckoned you hadn't seen it before."

He held up the film.

I didn't recognise it, so I shook my head.

"Great!" He threw the film at me and I barely

managed to catch it. "Power that up and I'll get a bowl for the crisps. Do you want a glass for the beer or do you want to drink from the bottle?"

"The bottle." I got up to turn the telly on and put the disc in the Blu-ray player.

He emptied the bag of crisps into a bowl as I clicked on the proper choices for sound and subtitles.

"Tell me something," he said.

I slowly turned to him.

He quirked an eyebrow at me and grinned. "Is there something going on between you and and that boyfriend's of Andreas? You've been hanging out pretty often the past couple of months."

"Blokes can be friends, you know." I opened one of the beer bottles and handed it to him, then opened a second one for myself. "Not everybody ends up in bed together."

"Sure." Tarjei dropped down on one side of the sofa and took a long swallow of the beer. "But you're without a boyfriend and he's without a boyfriend… I'm just saying, it gets lonely."

I narrowed my eyes at him. "He's not a cheater. Neither am I."

Alex was just a friend; there was absolutely nothing else going on. We understood each other, but we weren't attracted to each other.

Sure, Alex was easy on the eyes, but he was

Andreas' boyfriend. If I hadn't been in love with someone else, I still wouldn't have made a move on him.

"You and I are friends, Tarjei" I pointed out dryly. "We've never ended up in bed."

"True. But that doesn't mean I'd say no if the opportunity presented itself."

Now he was taking the piss out of me.

I didn't deign to answer him.

Instead I started the film and took another gulp of beer. He must've come over right from the shop; the bottle was still cold.

The film was just starting up when my doorbell rang again.

I frowned over at Tarjei.

Alex had been by earlier in the day, and I couldn't see a reason he'd be back. He'd been heading off to meet another friend of his. And I couldn't possibly imagine that Daniel would come over for a chat on a Saturday evening either.

I walked over to the door and opened it slowly.

"Jørgen."

Geir turned towards me with a wide smile.

He had a bag slung over one shoulder, and his other arm was raised in a wave.

I lifted my head enough to spot Nik's car

speeding down the street, then I turned my full focus back to him again.

"Geir." I had no idea what to say. What was he doing on my porch?

Geir's wide smile fell into a wry, teasing one. "Have you forgotten about my holiday?"

"But…" I wracked my brain. "The holiday isn't until next week." Alex was only back in town for the weekend. He had another week of lectures before he came for the Autumn holiday.

"Here, maybe. In Oslo it's this week."

I took him in.

His hair was slightly shorter than it had been before he'd left, but it was still long. It still fell around his face and into his eyes. He wore a T-shirt and form-fitting jeans and his Converse.

He looked exactly like I remembered him, but there was something more confident about him, about that smile, about the look in his eyes.

"Aren't you going to let me in?" He cocked his head to the side. He said it teasingly, but his eyes had a guarded look to them now.

"Of course." I stepped aside quickly, letting him brush past me inside.

I swallowed my sudden nervousness at his presence. I'd been talking to him over the phone for the past three months, and now here he was in the flesh.

Right in front of me.

I could reach out and touch him and he'd actually *be* there for me to hold on to.

I'd only taken one step towards him when he was in my space, arms wrapping around my neck as he hugged me tight. "I've missed you so much, Jørgen," he whispered against my neck.

I slid my arms around his back, hugging him just as tightly as he hugged me.

I was still shocked that he was there, in my arms. I'd been so set on the holidays being next week.

We'd never actually spoken of any particular dates, but now that he mentioned it, I did know that the southern parts of the country had their holiday a week before we did.

It was a complete surprise to have him there, but it was an extremely pleasant one.

I could feel his body through his shirt. He'd filled out a bit since the last time I saw him. He wasn't quite as skinny anymore—he had gained more defin-ition. He must be eating better now that he had a whole family around him to take care of him.

"It's so good to see you again." His breath tickled my skin, causing goose bumps to pop up across my neck.

"Yeah. You too."

I finally let him go and he stepped back to look up

at me again. His green eyes were sparkling with happiness, and I drew in a quick breath as I realised it was because of *me*.

Because he was finally back here with me.

If that wasn't an ego booster, I didn't know what was.

"Come on in. Tarjei and I are watching a film." I motioned towards the sofa, where Tarjei had his head buried in his mobile.

I suspected he was trying to give us our privacy.

He must've heard everything, since he'd paused the film when I'd got up to answer the door.

Geir toed out of his Converse and followed me as I headed over to the sofa. Tarjei looked up, gaze instantly zeroing in on Geir with interest.

No, not interest, per se, maybe more curiosity?

He had only met Geir that one time, when I'd told him to go away, after all, so he must be curious about him.

"Hi. I'm Tarjei." He held his arm out to Geir, who shook it with a shy smile. "Want a beer?"

"Oh, no thanks."

"He's seventeen," I said at the same time as Geir declined.

Geir turned his shy smile on me. "I'll just get a glass of water." He turned and headed over to the kitchen.

Tarjei arched his eyebrows teasingly at me while Geir had his back turned to us.

I narrowed my eyes at him. I didn't trust Tarjei with Geir; I had no control over what he might say. Something embarrassing, for sure, if he was given the opportunity. He didn't always filter himself when he talked.

He only quirked his eyebrows higher, gave a shit-eating smile, and I turned away from him to look at Geir as he sat down next to me. He didn't sit close, not so close we touched, but he was closer to me than I was to Tarjei.

"Ready?" Tarjei lifted the remote.

He pressed play and the film started right in the middle of an explosion. The thing with action flicks was that there was always something going on, even if the plot itself was rather unoriginal and dull. There were explosions, gun firing scenes, chase scenes... so the time flew past.

Tarjei and I finished the six-pack of beer during the movie, and all three of us finished up the crisps.

Tarjei left shortly afterwards, obviously to give us our privacy.

He grinned at me one last time, and actually *winked* before he headed out the door.

I carried the empty bottles to the kitchen to sort them with the rest of the bottles I had gathered, then

I went back to sit on the sofa where Geir was curled up.

"Hey," I said, suddenly not able to take my eyes off of him.

He looked so good, healthy and happy. The sadness from our last month together, after the loss of Charo, was undetectable now. I knew he still missed Charo, but the grief wasn't all-consuming anymore.

"Hey," he replied, staring back at me.

I don't know which one of us moved first.

Maybe we moved at the same time.

All I knew was that we were kissing, and I realised I had missed it quite a lot.

Kissing had never been a part of my life before him; he'd been my very first kiss and I hadn't kissed anyone *but* him. I didn't want to kiss anyone else.

His lips fit perfectly against mine. They were soft and warm, and his body was hard but willing as he leaned against me.

"Are you doing all right?" he asked me when he did pull apart.

He stayed where he was, leaning against me, but he did cock his head a little back and to the side so he could look at me. "You can disguise your tone on the phone, but I can see you now."

"I'm doing better," I replied. I wasn't doing all

right, far from it, but I wasn't as bad as I'd used to be either.

Anxiety had lessened, probably thanks to the medication.

The flashbacks didn't happen as often, and Gina said that was thanks to me finally starting to come to terms with my past.

The panic attacks happened less too. That might have been the therapy and medication. I didn't know, but it was a guess.

We'd finally found a medication that worked for me without making me feel like shit, or not feeling anything at all, so all in all I was doing quite better.

"Good." He leaned in close to nuzzle my cheek. "I've missed you so much."

I wrapped my arms around him again. "Are you doing all right? School's still going okay?"

He enjoyed his new school more than he had enjoyed school here. He'd got to know a few of his classmates, but none of them were close friends to him like Nikolai had become.

"It's boring doing only general studies, but yeah, it's going okay. I can't wait for the year to be over, though." His arms slid around my neck as he put his head down to rest on my shoulder.

"Have you met anyone special?" I'd meant what I'd said when he'd left. I wanted him to do normal teenage stuff. Whatever that might entail, I wanted him to live his youth.

I didn't want to tie him down.

He was young, he didn't have any experience, and I didn't want to stand in the way of the typical teenage stuff that I'd never been able to do. Especially as I wasn't sure I could give him everything he deserved.

"Yeah. I met him back in January. But he's obviously oblivious."

"Cheeky." I couldn't help the smile that forced its way across my lips. "I meant what I said to you." I buried my face in his hair. It was soft and smelled of lavender.

"I know." His arms tightened around my neck. "Nik thinks I should totally take advantage of it. But, frankly, you're the only one I can think about."

"Maybe if you were open for it—"

"Are you trying to get rid of me?"

"No. I'm not. I just want you to live a little. You live in Oslo now, there's so many choices there. You can do so much you've never had the chance to do here. You can do so much better."

"Don't." He buried his face in my neck. "Don't say that. You're *good*. I'm not ever going to be promiscuous like Nik, or out and proud like him. That's not me. In fact, I don't really have much interest in such things at all. All I want is to finish the year and come back home."

"How can that not be of interest to you?" I asked hoarsely. "Every teenager—"

"I'm not like every teenager. It might just be the way I'm made or it might be my medication. I don't know. All I know is that I want to come home. I want to come home to *you*."

And who was I to argue?

That was all I wanted too.

PART III
YOU CAN CALL IT LOVE

GEIR

CHAPTER 10

"What do you mean we're not going home for Christmas?"

Dad looked at me, expression set. "I mean exactly that. We're not going home for Christmas. *This* is our home now."

"You promised me we'd go home every holiday, Dad!"

I'd heard him say it to Charlotte as I descended the stairs, that we were celebrating Christmas here.

My hands shook. I was that upset.

"You said that yourself!"

"I changed my mind." Dad crossed his arms over his chest. "As I said, *this* is our home now. Daniel, Carina, and Marika are coming down here to celebrate with us. Martin and Linnea will be here too. It'll be nice."

"The fuck it will!" I didn't realise until Dad's eyes narrowed that I'd been swearing. "Every holiday, that's what you said to me. Guess what? Christmas is a holiday!"

"This isn't up for discussion. We're staying here."

"You can stay here. I'm going *home*."

"You're not going anywhere. Your home is with me!" He was getting angry now too.

I didn't care.

He was the one in the wrong here. He'd gone back on his word, on something he had promised me before we'd even moved.

"I don't want to stay with someone who *lies*!"

For the first time in my life I felt like hitting something.

Preferably him.

I didn't. I only curled my hands into fists and turned on my heels.

"Arsehole!" I slammed the kitchen door closed so hard it rattled.

How could he, once again, refuse me to go home to visit? He'd refused me at the end of the summer holidays, and now he was doing it again.

I was pretty sure he would've refused me to go back for the autumn holiday too, since he'd opted to stay in Oslo, but I'd caught a ride with Nik and left before he could say anything to me.

What was Dad's deal? Why was he still so against Jørgen? Even after everything I'd told him back when we'd driven down to Oslo…

Grabbing my shoulder bag, I stepped into my beat-up Converse and exited the house.

I didn't slam the front door. I wanted to, I really did, but I had already slammed one, no need to abuse another one.

I put on my headphones as I waited for the bus, and wrapped my arms around myself as I fumed. I should've put on more clothes. It was cold in December. But I wasn't going back, so what I had on would have to do.

The bus stopped in front of me and I stepped on it. I scanned my card, saw I still had twelve days left, then found a seat facing the right way. I hated sitting the wrong way.

I wanted to go back home so I could see Jørgen again. It had been one and a half months since I'd seen him. The autumn holiday had only been a week, and I'd been looking forward to over two whole weeks for Christmas.

Then Dad decided to be an arse and not go home like he'd promised.

It was half an hour until my doctor's appointment, so I was early, and I curled up in a chair in the waiting room and drew my notebook out of my bag.

I didn't think I'd ever send this letter to Jørgen. I was too angry to articulate myself properly, but getting the words down on paper helped me calm down. I'd written four pages of ranting about Dad and had started a calmer letter that I hoped to be able to send to him when my name was finally called.

I'd been to see the doctor several times since moving, so he was familiar. That didn't mean I was any more comfortable, though, especially with what I was going to talk to him about.

"So what can I help you with today?" he asked, smiling kindly at me. He was middle-aged and specialised in epilepsy. That was why my previous doctor back home had referred me to him. No doctor back home had epilepsy as their specialty, so back then I'd had to go to Oslo or Trondheim for serious check-ups.

"Well." I blew out a breath, wondering how to articulate myself. "I think my medication is ruining my sex drive." I said it in one long breath, so I wouldn't stop to filter myself.

His expression didn't change at all. He'd probably heard that a good many times. "Are you sexually active?"

"No. But I'd like to be." Preferably with Jørgen,

even if he seemed to think he couldn't give me everything I needed. I could only surmise that that meant sexually.

I, however, had faith.

I knew he liked me.

This was the natural progression of the relationship. I didn't expect anything to happen at Christmas, that wasn't why I'd made the appointment, but maybe by the time I finally moved back home.

Maybe then we'd both be ready to take the next step.

"Have you tried? To become sexually aroused?"

I nodded slightly. "I can get maybe half-hard, but that's it. It doesn't happen. I'm afraid it's the medication doing it, since that's a side effect. I've been on it for years, and I haven't been interested in… you know, before."

Or it could just be me. Maybe I didn't have it in me to have sex.

Then Jørgen and I would surely fit well together.

He asked me more questions, and I answered to the best of my ability. As I wasn't yet eighteen, he did need to inform Dad about a change of medication, so he rang him up.

I sat sullenly in front of him, still angry with Dad. The doctor didn't give the reason why I needed to change my medication, because he still had the confidentiality, even if I was seventeen.

Dad agreed, and the doctor printed out new prescriptions for me as well as several sheets of paper with information. He walked me through everything too, just to be certain.

We scheduled another appointment, after I'd been on the new medication for a couple of weeks.

I'd been used to taking my current meds only once a day, but now I had to take them twice. It was going to be quite a change, but I hoped certain things would improve.

I only hoped my seizures wouldn't get worse.

Dad was in the living room when I got home. My first instinct was to walk right past without speaking to him. Then again, he didn't like confrontations, so he wouldn't be bringing the subject up anytime soon.

"You said when we moved here I could go back during the holidays." I crossed my arms over my chest and leaned against the doorframe. I wasn't going to go further into the room, because if things turned bad I wanted to be able to head upstairs without having to cross the room and have him watch me while I did so.

"This is our first Christmas together as a family." He was both frustrated with me and almost begging with me to understand. "Our new family. You belong here with us."

I could see his point. Of course he'd like to spend Christmas in his new home, with his new girlfriend.

But he had to understand that I didn't want the same thing he did. I wanted Jørgen. He was important for my Christmas.

I snubbed my toe against the floor, a thought popping into my mind. "Why can't Jørgen come here, then?"

"Geir." He sighed.

I knew it wasn't going to happen.

"You're being unfair!" Why was he so set on making Christmas hell for me?

"You can see him next holiday. Easter. It's not that far off, only a few months. But Christmas... We're staying here."

I sniffled. "He's done nothing but be kind to me and look out for me. And he does a better job at it than you do." I hightailed it out of the room before he could see me crying.

He didn't follow me, and for that I was grateful. I was upset, and I needed him to leave me alone.

WE DIDN'T SPEAK much to each other after that.

He tried to speak to me, to be even nicer than he usually was, but I wasn't having it.

I didn't speak to him unless it was necessary, and when he went back to work I was grateful. I was so angry with him for keeping me back in Oslo for the holiday, I needed time away from him. That he worked offshore was great for that.

Christmas was soon upon us.

I hadn't thought about it before, but now that Charlotte stressed around to get everything in order for our visitors, I became aware of the fact that there weren't enough rooms for everyone.

Uncle and Aunt got the only available guest room, and Charlotte decided to have Marika and Linnea bunk with Marlene in her room and to put Martin in mine.

I wasn't pleased about this, because he didn't speak to me. Like, *ever*. He could hardly look at me, and now I was expected to share a bed with him?

It wasn't like I could make him sleep on the floor. Though the thought was tempting.

I spent the day of their arrival in Oslo city centre with Nik, buying our last Christmas presents. He was leaving early the next morning, and I was jealous that he got to go home whereas I had to stay.

Dad came home the next day too, because he'd

made sure he'd got Christmas off this year, with it being his first year living with Charlotte and all.

"Will you give this to Jørgen for me?" I reached in my shoulder bag and drew up a package. It was wrapped in shiny blue and silver paper with a silver bow on top next to where I'd written *to Jørgen*.

"That looks nice." Nik took the package from me gently.

"I spent an awful long time wrapping it. I had to make sure it was perfect."

"It is." Nik placed it into one of his many bags. "I'll make sure he gets it."

"Thank you."

"Can I ask what it is?" Nik lifted the arm that was holding most of the bags up and down a couple of times. "It weighs a bit."

"I can't. Not yet. I'll tell you when you get back after New Year's." I grinned at him. I didn't think Nik would tell Jørgen what it was, but I wanted it to stay a secret until Jørgen had opened it. I wanted him to be the first person to know what it was.

"I'll hold you to that." Nik kissed my cheeks in farewell, and I hurried over to catch my bus.

I met Kristoffer in the kitchen when I got home. He straightened up from the fridge and closed it with a snap.

"Anyone home?" I asked.

He turned to me and shook his head. "Mum's not home from work yet. Linnea and Martin came over earlier, and Linnea went out with Marlene."

I raised my eyebrows. "And where's Martin?"

"In the living room." He pointed his thumb over his shoulder, towards the door leading to said room. "Can you keep him company? I don't have time."

"What're you so busy with?"

"Stuff," he said as he exited the kitchen. I heard him run up the stairs.

I sighed and cast a glance at the closed door.

Martin didn't like me.

He certainly never talked to me. Hardly ever looked at me.

How was I supposed to keep him company? It would leave us both uncomfortable. But then again we would have to share a room, share a *bed*, even, as we didn't have an extra one. My bed was big, but still…

I'd only ever shared a bed with Jørgen.

And Charo, but a pet didn't count.

Tonight was going to be awkward.

Maybe spending time with him now, before anyone else came home would be a good idea. Maybe he'd loosen up a bit. He was very uptight. He never said much at all.

I sighed again, then went into the living room.

Martin was curled up on the sofa with his nose in a book. He didn't so much as move when I came into the room.

"Hi," I said as I sat down in the armchair.

He jerked, looked up, blushed, and looked back down at his book. He didn't even answer me.

What was wrong with him?

What was wrong with *me*?

I'd hoped I wouldn't feel like this again when I moved. But here I was, feeling excluded and alone, exactly like school had made me feel for my entire life. Some people just wouldn't give me a chance before dismissing me. That hurt.

"We're sharing a room," I said. "Do you want me to show you where it is so you can drop off your stuff?" I suspected he had brought stuff with him, though I couldn't see a bag or a suitcase.

Martin nodded briefly. He produced a bookmark and carefully marked his book, then clutched it in one hand as he stood up.

I preceded him upstairs.

His bag had been by the front door, and I'd walked right past it earlier. He put it down on the foot of my bed, which he eyed warily.

"Don't worry," I told him, perhaps a bit more harshly than I'd intended, "it's a big bed. It's not like you'll catch anything."

He cast a startled look at me. "What?"

I shrugged and looked away. Why was he so uncomfortable around me? I had never done anything to turn him against me.

"Make yourself at home." With that I went back downstairs.

THE REST of the day went by in a blur. Charlotte came home from work, and I helped her make dinner. She was stressed because my family was arriving and Dad still wasn't home.

He came home the next day, which meant that Charlotte had to greet our family all alone.

I felt for her, so I helped with dinner and I set the table while she went upstairs to shower and change.

Marlene and Linnea had come home while I'd been in the kitchen, and they were watching television in the living room. Martin was back to his book, curled on the other end of the sofa from where Linnea sat.

I didn't join them. I went up to my room to finish another letter to Jørgen.

I'd started doing sketches in the letters now, sketches of just random things, but I hoped he liked them.

I was currently working on a sketch of Charo, which took up half a page.

This would be my first Christmas in eleven years without him.

I looked up at the urn, which I'd put on top of the shelves over my desk. It was hard, but it wasn't as hard as it had been in the beginning. Nor as hard as I'd imagined it would be. Maybe because I wasn't at home, where I had all my memories of him. Charo had never set paws in Charlotte's house, so he didn't belong here. Maybe it would've been harder for me to go home for Christmas, considering.

Jørgen would've made it better, though; he always did.

I turned my focus back on the sketch. I had to get Charo's collar just right. The collar I'd secured around the urn, just to be certain I wouldn't lose it.

I managed to finish the sketch before I heard commotion downstairs. I hurried down and smiled widely at seeing my uncle, aunt, and cousin. I hugged them in turn, happy to see them.

It wasn't their fault my Christmas was ruined—it was probably Dad who'd invited them out of spite so he'd have an excuse not to go back home.

There were introduction all around.

Charlotte had met them before, back when she'd visited last Easter holiday, but the rest of them had never met. I noticed how Martin seemed much more comfortable greeting them, he even shook their hands. He hadn't done that with me.

"How are you doing?" Uncle Daniel wrapped an arm around my shoulders as Charlotte shooed everyone else into the dining room for dinner. "I'm sorry you weren't able to go home. I know you were looking forward to it."

I stared up at him. He was taller than me, just as tall as Jørgen.

"Dad's doing this to me on purpose." It sounded petulant, but I couldn't help it.

"Your dad wants to spend Christmas in his own home, this home, with his girlfriend and the combined family." Daniel smiled. He always saw something good in every situation. I didn't know if it was his training as a psychiatrist or if it was just him as a person, but sometimes it could be really annoying.

"How is Jørgen?" I asked. I didn't want to talk about Dad anymore.

Daniel pressed his lips together in thought. "He's doing better."

"He keeps telling me that too. Better than what, though? Better than he was when we met? Or better for every single time he says it?"

"He's working through some major stuff. Give him time." Daniel squeezed my shoulders.

"I have given him time. I mean, I *am* giving him time. It would be nice to just once in a while know a little more than *better*, you know."

"It's hard for him. Be patient." Uncle clapped my shoulder as he preceded me into the dining room.

I stared after his back for a moment before I followed.

I took a seat next to Marika at the end of the table. I was happy to see them all again. I'd only checked in with them briefly during autumn holiday, since it had only been for a week and I'd wanted to spend as much time as possible with Jørgen.

CHAPTER 11

*D*inner was nice.

Charlotte was an excellent cook, and Aunt kept complimenting her for it. Charlotte promised she'd give her the recipe. It was a late dinner, but we tended to have that on Saturdays. Still, they'd driven all the way from back home in a day, and they were knackered.

Charlotte showed Uncle and Aunt to their guest room, and Marlene and Linnea disappeared upstairs with Marika. Kristoffer slinked off to his room, which he was allowed to stay in by himself. Why couldn't Martin bunk with *him* though? They were the ones who were related after all.

So now I was left alone with Martin.

We didn't say a single word to each other.

Charlotte thankfully came back downstairs after a few minutes, and my aunt and uncle followed a while later.

We all spent the evening in front of the television. Only they were actually watching it; Martin had his nose buried in that book again, and I was sketching.

I went to bed first, not because I was tired, but because I wanted to fall asleep before Martin. Trouble was, I couldn't seem to fall asleep, as I kept tossing and turning for the next hour.

When I heard footsteps near my door, I turned towards the wall before he entered. I managed to lie quietly, but I still wasn't even close to being tired.

I heard him shuffling behind me, then he slowly and as quietly as possible got into bed besides me. We weren't lying close, it was a double bed, after all, and I was lying pretty close to the wall. Still, I was acutely aware that he was there and that he was uncomfortable.

I wasn't any more comfortable myself.

"Why don't you like me?" I hadn't meant to say it out loud, and the fact I had left me mortified.

It was out there now, however, and maybe it was just as well.

I couldn't sleep like this, so maybe we'd actually figure out a way to deal with each other. Or we might not and I would go down to sleep on the sofa.

Rather the sofa than here being all tense and uncomfortable.

"Kristoffer said you were gay."

It didn't surprise me that that was the issue.

So Kristoffer had been gossiping about me. Didn't surprise me either.

"It's not contagious," I snapped in a low voice. "It's not like I'm going to molest you." I turned onto my back so I could throw a glance over at him.

He was on his back as well, staring up at the ceiling.

"I don't think you will," he murmured.

"Then what's your problem? I'm gay. I've got epilepsy. Neither is about to change, whichever it is that bothers you."

I'd been treated as an outsider all my life because of, mostly, my disease. But also because of my sexuality, especially the last part of second year in school, when Jonas' had it confirmed that I was gay.

If there was anything Nik had changed in me the last few months, it was that I wasn't about to take shit from anyone about who I was. I wasn't going to be ashamed.

He *never* took shit and he was vocal about it when someone did take issue. Nik was himself to the fullest, and that was what I admired the most about him.

TT KOVE

"It doesn't bother me. Any of it." He moved around a bit, I assumed to find a better position.

Except he moved closer to me—and I didn't even have a chance to process that before his lips pressed against mine.

I tensed up in surprise, maybe even shock, because what the hell?

I thought he didn't like me and here he was kissing me! His lips were soft, fuller than mine or Jørgen's, but they felt nice. His body, too, was warm where it was stretched out next to me.

I put my hands on his chest, pushing away a bit. "What are you doing?"

"I'm sorry," he whispered and I could tell from the weak light shining in the window that his face was bright red.

Here I'd been, thinking he didn't like me at all, when the truth was quite the opposite.

Well, colour me surprised.

I'd actually judged him, like so many had judged me, without digging any deeper.

I felt an extreme bout of guilt just then.

"No, *I'm* sorry," I said, hoping my voice was as honest as I wanted it to be. "I'm sorry I never bothered trying to get to know you. That I've been dismissive. That wasn't nice of me. I know what it's like to be dismissed like that, and I never wanted to do it to someone else, but it seems I have."

"It's okay." He propped himself up on an elbow, and he stared down at his arm as he spoke. "I haven't exactly been open to it, either."

I couldn't see his eyes in the dark, but I could tell he was still embarrassed.

"I've only ever kissed one other person," he whispered.

"Something we have in common then, because so have I." His cheek had brushed mine when he kissed me, and I reached out, without even thinking about it, to trace my finger over it.

With Jørgen, there was usually a bit of stubble, unless he'd shaved the same day. Martin's cheek was smooth, exactly like mine. His skin was a bit rougher than mine, but not by much.

"Kristoffer said you had a boyfriend." Martin lifted his head slightly to look at me.

I nodded. "I do." Jørgen was my boyfriend, and it was going to stay that way.

And speaking of Jørgen... He'd told me to enjoy myself when I was in Oslo. Was this what that entailed? He wanted me to gain some experience, experience besides him.

To do whatever he hadn't been able to do.

"Will your boyfriend mind?" Martin's brows drew together in a frown.

"Mind what?"

"That I kissed you."

Jørgen's words flashed through my head, and I slowly shook my head. "No. I don't think he will." Jørgen wanted me to get experience… Did he want me to have some before we did anything?

So I'd know what to do when we got that far?

It wasn't like Martin was ugly. Now that I knew he liked me, as opposed to what I'd thought before, I could see he was cute. Maybe even just as inexperienced as I was?

"I don't mean to ruin anything between you and your boyfriend. I just—I like you. I didn't know how to say it, so I kissed you." His voice got lower and lower the more he talked, and the last two words were spoken in such a low whisper I had a hard time catching them.

Experience, experience, experience. The word was on repeat in my head.

"I love Jørgen."

"Yeah." He looked at me, startled at my intensity.

He wants me to enjoy myself. To get some experience. Maybe that would work in my favour when I finally did get to see Jørgen again?

Maybe if I wasn't such a complete virgin when it

came to everything, he'd be more open towards making our relationship physical? If I didn't get to see him again until February, I would be eighteen.

Maybe that would make him feel better about it too.

"I guess if you want to kiss me again, it would be okay."

I hoped.

Or maybe I misunderstood everything all together. Maybe he'd just meant enjoy myself without intimacy? I couldn't remember if he'd said that exact word or not. But he *had* said experience, and what else could experience mean?

"You sure?" He scooted closer again.

I wasn't.

Not at all.

But... Martin was here, he was willing. He was cute. I could definitely gain some experience right then are there.

"Yeah."

He hesitated for a moment, but then he did lean in.

And this time I kissed him back.

MARTIN WASN'T as uncomfortable around me after our night of snogging in my bed.

But as soon as I woke up the day after, my stomach had been knotted in a big ball of regret.

It wasn't made any better by Dad's arrival home, considering I was still angry with him. In a sense, it was his fault I'd snogged Martin the night before, because if he'd allowed me to go home where I *belonged*, it never would've happened.

Marika left right after Christmas, as she had to work. But my uncle and aunt were staying, as were Martin and Linnea. This meant that Martin still had to share my bed.

I wasn't so sure what to think about it, because the kissing had been nice... while it happened anyway. But it wasn't going to happen again. I didn't have any kinds of feelings towards Martin—except being happy he didn't hate me, and now regretting snogging him in the first place.

Maybe we could be friends? I couldn't give him any more than that.

Jørgen rang me the day after Marika left. It was weird seeing his name on my screen, as usually I was the one ringing him. I hadn't talked to him since before Christmas, so having him ring me made my stomach do flip-flops.

I went up to my room to take the call. I took the

stairs two at a time. "Hi," I breathed into the receiver as I shut my door behind me. I leant back against it, longing to hear his voice again.

"Hey." I could hear him breathing on the other end. "Are you doing all right?"

He always asked me that. "Yeah. I am." I gripped my mobile tighter. "Are you?" Maybe he had a reason for calling me.

"Just wanted to hear your voice," he said in a low voice, and that simple sentence practically made my knees buckle. I slid down to sit on the floor.

"Do you miss me?" I couldn't help but ask.

I wanted to hear the answer put out there in words.

"More than you'll ever know," he whispered.

I didn't even know how to reply to that. It made me happy, giddy, and every other synonym related to those two.

"Did you like my Christmas present?" I'd been worried about it, which was partly the reason I hadn't rung him yet. The other was that with visitors here I was also busy during the days, so I hadn't found the time.

I'd been longing to talk to him, however, and it felt so good to finally be able to.

"I did. Thank you." He breathed quietly for a bit. "I hung it up in the bedroom."

"Really?"

When I'd been back for autumn holiday, I'd managed to take a picture of us together. Self-taken, of course, because he wasn't about to let anyone else take a picture of us out in public.

The picture had turned out better than I'd ever imagined though, so the first part of his Christmas present was a framed copy of that photo. The second part, the bigger part, was the painting I'd done to replicate the photograph. It hadn't been a big painting, only A4, but I had framed that as well.

I'd been ridiculously nervous about it all. Pictures had seemed a bit lame to give someone for Christmas, but I knew he missed me, and I'd hoped that actually having something to look at would make him feel better.

"I did, yeah." He was silent for a moment, but I could hear a small commotion at his end.

"What's going on?" I strained my ears to hear, but I had no idea what it could be. Did he have someone over to visit? Tarjei, maybe.

"I…Well. I got a dog."

"A dog?" *He* had got a dog. "Why?"

Silence. Then in a whisper, "I didn't want to be alone anymore."

I closed my eyes. I wanted to be there with him, wanted to be there *for* him. If only Dad hadn't gone and decided on moving to Oslo without even so much as talking to me…

It wouldn't do much to be bitter about it, though. It wouldn't make time speed up, wouldn't make me finish school any faster so I could go home.

"Why a dog?" My eyes involuntarily rose to stare at Charo's urn and sadness welled up inside me.

"I don't know. I knew how much you loved Charo, and how much he kept you company. Then when I saw the ad in the paper… it seemed like a good idea."

"When'd you get him?"

"After the autumn holiday. I didn't know how to tell you. I know you're still broken up over Charo, and I just… I don't know. I didn't want you to be sad."

I couldn't be annoyed when he put it like that, not even if I'd wanted to.

"Do you like having a dog?"

"It takes some getting used to." He chuckled. "But yeah. He's good company."

I could hear my name being called from downstairs.

I groaned a bit.

We were going out for dinner today, but did we have to go right now? I wanted to talk to Jørgen.

"Charlotte's calling for me." I knew he could hear

the disappointment in my voice. "Can I ring you tomorrow? We haven't talked much lately. I miss talking to you."

"You can call whenever you want."

He sounded a bit melancholy.

"Are you okay, Jørgen?" I hated not being able to see him or touch him. To not comfort him.

"I had a pretty hard session with Gina today. She's working between Christmas and New Year's, thankfully. Still… It's just hard, you know?"

My name was called again.

I tried to shut it out.

"If you ever need to talk to someone else, you know I'm here, right? I'll always listen to what you have to say."

I heard him sigh. "I know. I just… I don't think I want you to know everything, to be honest. I don't want you to feel sorry for me or look at me any differently."

"Whatever you need," I whispered, and I meant it. If he didn't want to talk to me, that was fine. If, however, he should want to, I'd gladly be there for him.

He was quiet for a second. "Thank you."

We hung up, and I gripped my mobile tight for a moment before I sighed and finally pushed up on my feet.

My name was called a third time as I exited my room.

I hurried down the hallway and started down the stairs. I could see Charlotte at the bottom of them, looking up at me.

"I'm coming, I'm com—"

Someone yelled my name, but then the darkness swallowed me completely.

CHAPTER 12

*M*y eyes blinked open to bright lights. I closed them again.

Then I tried to move, but my body was sluggish and something was weighing my left arm down.

I groaned as pain lanced through my body, and I opened my eyes again, slower this time around.

When the light didn't hurt me anymore, I looked to my side. I couldn't find the strength to lift my head yet.

Dad was in a chair next to my bed. His foot tapped against the floor, like he was in a hurry but unable to move.

"Dad." My voice was raspy. I wanted water.

He jerked in surprise and his head lifted up to stare at me. He took a glass that had been standing on the table next to me and held the straw to my lips. I was grateful for the straw, because I couldn't lift my head. My whole body *ached*.

"How are you feeling?" he asked, sounding anxious.

"Hurting." I swallowed another sip of water. "My whole body's hurting."

"You had a seizure right in the middle of the stairs. You fell down. It wasn't pretty." His free hand hovered in the air above me, like he wanted to touch me but didn't know if he should or could.

Oh God. I'd fallen down the *stairs*.

"What's the damage?" There had to be some, as my body wasn't at all happy.

"You broke your arm. That's the worst of the injuries. Otherwise it was just bruises. Really ugly bruises, but they'll heal a lot quicker than your arm will."

Oh no, not my arm! "Which one?"

"Left." Dad smiled slightly. "A bit of luck, at least."

I wanted to nod, but my neck wouldn't cooperate. I closed my eyes instead as I took several deep breaths. My left arm wasn't a disaster, though it would be a bitch to do stuff from now on.

I guessed Dad was right; at least it hadn't been

my right arm. If I hadn't been able to write or draw, I didn't know what I would've done.

"Geir…"

I opened my eyes again to look over at Dad. His voice shook. "What?"

"You had a status epilepticus." Dad kept folding and unfolding his hands. "You scared the hell out of Charlotte. She was sobbing by the time the ambulance got there. You scared me too, because you haven't had an SE in so many years. Maybe… maybe your medication isn't working? Maybe you should go back to the old one? The old schedule?"

Shit. An SE was not good. Either I had one long seizure that hadn't stopped after five minutes, or I'd had several of them in a row. I didn't even want to ask which one was the case.

"I—I don't think it's the medication."

I wanted to rub at my eyes, but one hand felt too heavy to lift and the other just flopped back down on the bed again.

I was *exhausted*.

"I've forgotten to take them at the scheduled time. I'm so used to once a day, in the morning, that I think I've forgotten to take the second dose several days in a row."

I closed my eyes again. How could I have been so stupid? I knew how important it was to take my medication. Yet now, when I thought about it, I knew I had forgotten several days in a row.

When I looked at Dad again, I could see him battling several emotions at once. Anger, probably at me for being so stupid, was the most dominant one, but there was also fear and relief.

"Why exactly did you want to change your medication? I know you still had seizures on it, but it kept most of them at bay, didn't it?"

I licked at my lips.

I couldn't tell him the reason!

It was too mortifying.

"Geir?"

"Dad." My brain frantically searched for other reasons I could've possibly wanted to change up my medication. The obvious one was to be rid of seizures altogether, but that was the reason he'd been given when I had first gone to the doctor.

"Geir." He set his face in a determined expression. His jaws even clenched. "Tell me, whatever it is."

"I can't. It's too— too embarrassing."

"I don't care. Tell me."

I wanted to pout, to pull a tantrum, but I was too old for that.

"I want to have sex." I rushed it out in one breath.

I could tell that caught Dad by surprise. He jerked back and his eyes widened. "Aren't you doing that already? I mean... you can't do that on your old dosage?" His face flushed red.

"I already told you Jørgen and I haven't done anything," I said quietly. "I couldn't—on the old medication, nothing really worked, you know? So... I needed to change it, to see if it was just me or if it actually was the medication."

"And?" Dad looked like he'd bitten into something sour. I bet I looked it too, because this was not a conversation I wanted to have with him.

"And it was the medication." Something had certainly been up last night. "I'm keeping with the new one, the new dosage. I guess I just have to set an alarm on my phone or something, so I won't forget the second one."

Dad ran a hand across his face. "This is more than I ever wanted to know."

"You're the one who demanded I tell you. So you only have yourself to blame."

"Are you doing this because of Jørgen?" He wouldn't look at me now. Instead he stared at a point over my head. "Is it because of him that you went to get your medication changed? Is he pushing you into—"

"Stop right there!" I wanted to hold up a hand, but my body still wasn't cooperating. "I can't deny that Jørgen doesn't have anything to do with this, because he does. Thing is, he doesn't know about it. He's my boyfriend, Dad, and I want to be with him in any way. When he's ready, I want to be ready."

Dad only stared at me.

"You have to trust me. You have to trust that I know what I want in life. That I don't do anything I don't want to do. Because I *don't*. No one's pushing me to do anything. I told you about Jørgen already. Being intimate is not something that's on the forefront of his mind at the moment, I can tell you that. But it is most likely going to happen. It's natural. He's the one I want to be with."

I had to make Dad understand.

"Why can't you see that? Why do you have to be so against it? Jørgen's good for me, and I'm good for him. I *love* him, Dad." I'd never said those words out loud to Dad, but that didn't make them any less true. "It hurts me that you can't accept that. That you're refusing me to go home so I can see him. You want to keep us apart, but it's not going to work, because I *am* going home this summer. I am going to be with him. I love him more than anything."

Dad still stared at me, but his eyes were more thoughtful now.

"You're so young—"

"I can still love someone. I can still know who I want to be with. From that day I met him, when I woke up in his flat after my seizure, I knew he was someone special. I *know* that he's the one for me. All I want is to be with him—and for you to accept that I'm with him. For you to accept *him*. Because he really is an amazing person. If you don't believe me, ask Uncle, because he knows too."

Dad fell silent again. He kept his head bowed so I couldn't see his expression.

When he lifted his head, his face was once again set, and I felt my stomach fall into knots.

"We're going to the cabin again this Easter, like we do every year. Charlotte and the kids are coming with as well. Why don't you invite Jørgen?"

"Really?" I knew my eyes were wide, but I'd been so certain he'd shoot me down again.

Dad didn't exactly look thrilled, but he nodded. "I mean it. Invite him. One lunch isn't enough to base my opinion on."

I felt like crying. "If I could actually move, I'd hug you."

"*I* can move." Dad smiled slightly, then bent over me and put his cheek to mine. He hesitated a moment with his arm, but then he wrapped them around me too.

My body protested, but I didn't mind.

Dad had relented some, and that was all I wanted.

So I lifted my right hand, with some difficulties, and put it on his back, hugging him awkwardly back.

～

JANUARY FLEW BY, and suddenly my eighteenth birthday was upon me.

My arm was still in a cast, which made some things a struggle, but I managed. As long as my right hand functioned, I could do most anything.

Dad and Charlotte gave me money for my birthday, so I could spend it on something I wanted. Uncle and Aunt gave me money too, but as they lived back home, they put the money into my bank account. Marlene got me some new paints, because I'd been using them a lot lately, while Kristoffer only acknowledged that it actually was my birthday. I didn't mind.

Martin too gave me a present, which surprised me. We'd met up after Christmas and New Year's, of course, but it wasn't like we were together. He liked me more than I liked him, and I didn't want to lead him on, so I kept him at a distance. The kisses we'd shared in my bed that night had been nice, but there'd been nothing else between us.

I'd felt he wanted there to be, but I couldn't do it. I didn't like him in that way.

And I still felt guilty over snogging him. I hadn't

told Jørgen about it though, because I had no idea *how* to tell him.

Martin's gift was a book. A book I had never heard about, not the title nor the author. I didn't read much, but when I looked at the back it turned out it was a gay romance, and my interest was piqued immediately. It was in English, but English was one of my favourite subjects, so that didn't deter me.

"Thank you." I hugged him then. I hoped that wouldn't lead him on.

Martin blushed, but he hugged me back.

He stayed around for dinner, but had to go home afterwards. It was just as well, because Nik was at my door right after Martin left. He had a bag in his hand and he grinned wickedly at me.

"Happy Birthday!" He kissed my cheeks, then brushed past me inside. We headed up to my room, where I closed my door firmly, because I definitely didn't trust that grin of his. "I got you something really special for your big eighteenth!" He thrust the bag at me.

I looked into it. There was one big package that was wrapped in red paper, and a small one wrapped in silver. I took out the small one first, threw him a suspicious glance, and opened it.

"Why are you giving me a bottle of lube?" I held

it up to look at. Water-based. Didn't really tell me much.

"Because you're going to need it." Nik put his hands on his hips and nodded towards the bag on the bed. "Open the big one!"

I was even more suspicious now and I took my time opening it. After rolling the gift out of the paper, I promptly dropped it on my bed. "Nik!"

He bent over laughing. "Oh my God, you should've seen your face!"

I stared from him, down to the plastic-wrapped item on my bed and back to him again. "I don't even —a *dildo*! Why in the world would you buy me a dildo?"

Nik laughed even harder. "Because everyone needs one, love. For practice, you know, or when there just isn't anyone interesting around and you have to take care of yourself."

My face burned, and I shoved the plastic wrapped dildo back into the bag together with the lube. "I can't believe you."

He dried tears from his eyes now, but he'd straightened up a bit.

I glared at him.

"Come on, love, don't be offended! I just saved you an embarrassing trip to a sex shop."

"You think it's embarrassing?"

"Oh god no. But *you* would've." He flicked his hand at me. "I am not embarrassed about my sexuality at all. You, on the other hand, are still a virgin. Handjobs and blowjobs are easy enough to get off on, but anal sex is something else entirely. It's, like, so bloody good. You *have* to try it."

"Not with a dildo." I could practically feel the steam erupting from my ears.

"Sex toys are *so* underrated." His laughter was gone, but that grin was still in place. "Sometimes I actually prefer my toys over a live cock. It depends on who the cock is attached to. If he's, like, a raging arsehole, I'd much rather do myself. There's no shame in that."

"Oh my God." I didn't even deign to answer that. "You're mental."

"I just really love sex." He raised his eyebrows suggestively. "I think you would as well."

I grimaced. "Can we *not* talk about this?"

Nik dropped it, thankfully, but he still looked at me with that mischievous sparkle in his eyes. He stayed for hours, and we hung out in my room—after I'd hidden the bag he'd given me under the bed so I wouldn't have to think about it.

Really, a *dildo*.

He wasn't right in the head.

I didn't want to lose my virginity to a *dildo*.

Did it even count as losing your virginity when it was a toy? Wasn't the whole point that you lost it once you'd had sex with another person?

"You are, you know. Mental." I couldn't quite let it go.

Nik only laughed. "Try it. Trust me, you'll *love* it."

I doubted it, but decided it was time to drop the subject entirely.

It didn't stop him from continuing to laugh at me though.

CHAPTER 13

*C*harlotte called us down a couple of hours after Nik's arrival, where she revealed she'd baked a cake for me.

I was pleasantly surprised. I hadn't expected a cake, or any fuss at all, but it was nice that she'd done it.

But when she carried it out into the living room, I found myself getting choked up.

"Carina gave me your mum's recipe," Charlotte said as she put it down in front of me. "She said she made this for you every birthday, and that she hated that she couldn't be here to do it this year. So… I did it." She smiled at me.

I couldn't get my voice to work, but I gave her a shaky smile.

It looked almost exactly like my aunt used to make it, and, as usual, it reminded me of my mum. I caught Dad staring at me, and I gave him a smile as well.

Charlotte cut up the first slice and put it on my plate, and I took a bite. It tasted exactly the same.

"This is great, Charlotte. Thank you." My voice was thick and everyone could hear it, but I didn't care. This was my mum's special recipe, and it had always been a yearly tradition on my birthday.

It meant more than I could say that Charlotte had gone to the trouble of make it for me.

We all enjoyed ourselves eating cake and drinking soda.

Nik left afterwards, and I retreated to my room.

I fell onto my bed, and felt like going straight to sleep, even if it wasn't that late, but there was still one thing I wanted on my birthday.

My mobile was on my bedside table. I was surprised to see I had a missed call, but I smiled when I saw who it was from. I rang back and waited in anticipation.

"There you are," Jørgen answered.

"Sorry I didn't answer. I was downstairs. Charlotte made my mum's special cake for me."

"Have you had a good day?"

"The best. Only one thing's missing." I closed my

eyes, listening to his voice. To think that it had already been over a year since I'd met him.

"What's that?" He sounded mildly curious.

"You." Seeing him was the only thing I hadn't got on my birthday. Everything else had been good, even Nik's embarrassing gift.

He chuckled.

I liked the sound of his voice. It was deep and it reverberated through me.

"Easter. You'll see me at Easter."

He'd said yes to coming to the cabin with us for a week. I longed to see him again, to kiss him, to hug him, to be in his mere presence.

I knew he had reservations about the entire holiday, but he'd still said yes. He'd said yes for me. Because I wanted him there, because I missed him and wanted to be with him. Because he missed me and wanted to be with me just as much as I did him.

"I can't wait," I whispered. "I can't wait to see you again."

A beat. "Me neither."

My heart started beating faster. The L-word was on the tip of my tongue, but I stopped myself. It was something that should be told in person, not over the phone. I wanted to see his reaction when I told him exactly how I felt.

"How's your day been?" I asked instead, bringing the focus from me over to him.

"Worked overtime today. There's a shop that's building out, so we were on a deadline to get the electrical up and running on the new section. Afterwards I went for a mountain hike with Nero."

Nero was his dog. I looked forward to meeting him too. I was starting to miss having a dog by now, but I still didn't want to get a new one. Not while living in Oslo. There weren't proper trails to go for a walk here, and certainly not hiking trips, unless I was willing to travel for quite some time to get to them.

"Was there much snow?" Oslo was the big city and it was inland, so it was freezing cold, but it didn't get a lot of snow.

"Not as much as it was this time last year."

"I'm looking forward to hiking with you and Nero at Easter. There's woods all around the cabin, so we can go in any direction without encountering much besides forest."

"That sounds nice." I could hear his doorbell ring over the short silence that fell between us. "That should be Alex." He'd told me about Alex, his cousin's boyfriend, whom he'd grown close to. I wasn't jealous, besides wishing it was me ringing his bell to spend time with him.

ANYTHING FOR HIM

"I'll let you go then. Have a good night." I didn't
want to let him go, but he was being sociable with
someone—and that was good.

"Happy Birthday, Geir," he said, voice low. "I
miss you."

"I miss you too." Usually I was the one who said
it first and he answered, and it made me happy that
he said it first this time.

We hung up, and I put my hand down on my
chest for a moment as I relived our conversation.

My eyes closed as I pictured him, how he'd
looked that day I left. How we'd kissed, and how his
arms had held me close. How it had felt to ring his
doorbell at Autumn holiday, the butterflies that that
gone wild in my stomach… and then how he'd
looked when he'd come to answer the door. How
he'd held me, how I'd clung to him, and then how
we'd kissed.

It was so long ago now, months, but I could still
picture it like it had happened yesterday.

And things happened down south—I got hard.

It happened more and more lately when I thought
about like this. When I pictured us intimate.

After the change in medication, and after remem-
bering to take the pills at the scheduled time, I could
finally get sexually aroused. It was weird, as I'd

never even touched myself before, but it was a good kind of weird.

It was embarrassing to think about touching myself, about pleasuring myself while I was all alone in my room. I'd much rather learn about my newfound sexuality with Jørgen, but alas... that wasn't possible.

My left hand was still in a cast, so I rubbed my groin through my jeans with my right one.

It wouldn't be long till I could take the cast off now. At the end of the month, if everything looked good.

After unbuttoning my jeans, I tentatively reached inside, rubbing over my half-hard erection again.

I'd never wanked off before.

But it was fitting that I wanted to try it today, on my eighteenth birthday.

Thoughts of Jørgen made me excited lately, but I'd ignored this part of my body until eventually it went away.

Not today.

I slipped my hand under my boxers, wrapping it around my dick. It was completely dry, and stroking it created a lot of friction.

I wished Jørgen would touch me like this, though he'd never seemed inclined to do more than hug or kiss me. He'd even said he might not be able to ever give me what I needed.

Still, he was the one I wanted.

My hand inched down, over my balls to the puckered hole I'd never dared touch before. What would it feel like to have Jørgen touch me there, to feel him push inside me?

I'd watched porn before, of course, but it had never done anything for me on my old dosage of medication. I knew what went on between two men, I knew exactly how they had sex and the mechanics of it. What I didn't know was how it would feel to actually have someone inside me.

They enjoyed it a lot in porn, and Nik did as well, at least according to himself.

Nik...

My gaze dropped to the floor.

I retracted my hand and reached under the bed to pull out the bag. After staring into it for a whole minute, I threw the lube on the bed. Lube was important.

I stared some more at the plastic-wrapped dildo, wondering if I dared do it. I wanted to feel it, and it was the obvious choice, but at the same time it wasn't a live dick. It wasn't Jørgen's.

It looked pretty lifelike, though. Nik liked using sex toys, and he wasn't even embarrassed about admitting it. What was stopping me from trying it out? Maybe I would like it as well.

My goal set, I sat up to open up the plastic. I struggled with it, because the edges were stuck together. I was contemplating finding some scissors when it finally opened up.

The flesh coloured dildo fell to the floor with a dull *thunk*.

I stared down at it.

Should I do this?

Yes.

Yes, I should.

It'd been packed up though, and probably smelled vile from it too. I needed to wash it. So I stuffed it into the bag, buttoned up my jeans again, then hurried across the hall to the bathroom where I thrust it under steaming water. I didn't want anything plastic-smelling anywhere near me, but I supposed hot water would clean it up enough.

When I was satisfied, I snuck back into my room, even if there wasn't anyone around to see me. I locked my door, something I hardly ever did.

Then I shucked my jeans and underwear, as well as my jumper and tee. They fell to the floor in a heap, but I couldn't care less. Now that I'd made up my mind, I was quite excited about trying the toy out. I wouldn't ever admit to Nik that I had tried it though, especially not on the very same day he'd given it to me.

He'd be so smug about it if I did—and I'd never hear the end of it.

With my left arm in a cast, I could only do one thing at a time. I had to flick the lube bottle open with the left hand, and I struggled to turn it and squeeze some out into my palm. I managed, eventually, and I wrapped my hand around my cock again, which had wilted a bit from my trip to the bathroom.

It filled with blood again as I stroked it, this time with lube to ease the friction.

I closed my eyes. I had a better time of imagining Jørgen if I did, and it certainly helped speed up the blood pulsing downwards. I bucked my hips up into my fist, imagining it was Jørgen's hand around me, that he was looking down at me and liking what he saw.

When I started to leak pre-come, I let go of my dick and slowly moved my hand down to *that* place. I circled my index finger around the pucker, not sure if I dared push it inside. It did feel good to touch it, and my finger slid around it easily by help of the lube.

I was relaxed and my body reacted in a nice way to my own attentions, so I gently put some pressure behind my index finger. I gasped slightly as it breached me, but not in pain.

It was a feeling I wasn't used to; it felt weird, but not exactly painful. More like just being *full*. I applied more pressure and my finger sank in to the second joint, then down to the knuckle. I moved it in and out for a bit, loosening myself.

It started feeling dry when I added a second finger, so I withdrew my hand to awkwardly squeeze some more lube out. I managed to kind of hold the bottle upside down with my injured arm, because while I couldn't move the actual arm and wrist, there was nothing wrong with my fingers except the fact that the cast was in the way of things.

Armed with more lube, I lay back down and put my fingers back *there* to slide into my body. Two this time, and with the generous amount of lube I'd applied, they slid in easily.

It was uncomfortable at first, as it had been with just the one, but I slowly got used to it—and it started to feel pleasurable. My cock was still hard even if it hadn't been given any attention in a while.

When three fingers slid easily into me, I eyed the dildo that rested on the bed next to me. It was both longer and thicker than my three fingers. Four fingers was an uncomfortable movement, so I finally retracted them to grab the dildo.

Again I had to struggle with the lube, and it was even worse now that I had to hold the dildo too. I managed to squeeze it out, and it slowly trickled down the length of it.

I used my fingers to spread the lube out over the entire toy. It glistened from the lube, and I stared at it as I contemplated what to do next. Lying down had been relaxing while I'd prepped myself, but as for actually using the dildo… I didn't think lying down would be the best thing to do.

Not the first time, anyway.

In the few porn films I'd watched, men seemed to prefer mounting their partner.

I held the dildo down with my uninjured hand as I positioned myself above it. I bit my lip in both anticipation and nervousness; this was something completely new. Something I'd never done before and it was *scary*.

I sat down until I could feel the head nudge my entrance. I tensed up a bit, then took several deep breaths to relax myself. I sat down further—and the head of the dildo pressed into me, breaching me.

It was a *lot* wider than my fingers and it burned, but I kept going. It was worse at first, maybe because of the mushroom-shaped head, but as I'd got past that I slid down the length much more easily.

I stopped to take more deep breaths as it buried

inside me. The dildo had balls, though they weren't as lifelike as the dildo itself. It also had a suction cup at the bottom, but that didn't work against my bedspread, so I kept holding on to it.

It was *big*.

What was Nik thinking?

Weren't there any smaller dildos?

Lifting myself up, I sank slowly back down again, and this time the head nudged against something inside me.

My prostate.

I couldn't stop the moan that erupted from the unexpected pleasure. I rose up and sank back down again, quicker than last time, and once again it rubbed that spot.

"Oh my *God*."

It felt so good, but my thighs weren't used to the position or the movements. They were starting to burn. It didn't really matter, because as the toy nudged my prostate on each downward thrust, it didn't take me long to finish.

For the first time ever, I came from anal penetration, without my cock even being touched once. I let go of the dildo to stroke myself dry, and when I was empty, I lifted myself up off it and lay back down on my back.

I stared up at the ceiling as I caught my breath.

Nik had been right. *So* right.

Anal sex *was* something else entirely.

Sex toys *were* underrated.

If a toy felt so good, how amazing would it be with the right person?

What would sex be like with Jørgen?

PART IV
YOU LIGHT UP MY WORLD

JØRGEN

hy did I say yes to this?

I stared up at the cabin in front of me. It wasn't the biggest cabin I'd passed on my way up the mountain, but it looked rather homey. There were curtains in every window, as well as flowers.

Probably fake ones, but they looked pretty all the same.

I wondered how we were all going to fit. There couldn't possibly be bedrooms enough for all of us.

The thought of having to share a bedroom with anyone but Geir made my anxiety kick up like it hadn't done in quite a while.

A black, cold nose thrust into the side of my face and a warm pink tongue flicked out to lick me.

I sputtered as I jerked back, then I pushed Nero's

curious face away. I glanced back at him, and his tail started wagging excitedly.

"Right, boy," I muttered. "Let's do this."

I got out of the car. The air was fresh but freezing, and I shuddered as I opened the back door to grab my thick winter jacket. Nero jumped out before I could even grab it, and he ran forward right into a shovelled pile of snow. I quickly donned my jacket and zipped it up over my knitted jumper.

I reached in next for my bag, hefted it up on one shoulder as I locked the car, then I headed up the driveway towards the front door. Snow crunched under my boots, but at least the driveway was shovelled and hard-packed.

Nero, on the other hand, was running in the deepest of the snow, getting himself all wet. I'd have to dry him off before he could venture inside.

The door opened before I reached it, and Geir stepped outside. His boots were on but unlaced, and he was dressed in jeans and a thick knitted jumper kind of like mine. His smile was wide, and my anxiety fell to the wayside at the sight of him.

I took the stairs in two jumps, dropped my bag, and threw my arms around him. "It's been too long," I whispered against his soft hair.

He clung to me, just as tightly as I held him. "I've

missed you so much!" His face buried against my neck and his eyelashes tickled my skin.

I ran my hands up his back to cup his neck with one and his cheek with the other. I tilted his head back, then bent down to kiss him. His lips were familiar, soft and warm and yielding under mine.

He kissed me back, now taking more control of it than he had before.

I didn't mind, not at all.

When he shuddered, did I took a step back. "Get back inside. You've got too little clothes on to be out here." I pushed him gently towards the door.

He turned in the doorway to wait for me as I picked up my bag and whistled for Nero, who was now rolling around in the snow.

"Do you have a towel for him? I can't let him in like this."

He nodded and disappeared for a minute, then came back holding a big fluffy towel. Nero came jumping up on the porch, shaking himself and sending snow everywhere.

Geir laughed behind me while I bent down to dry Nero off.

I was led inside once Nero was as dry as he was going to get. I hoisted my bag on my shoulder after getting out of boots and jacket.

Geir walked close to me, so close our arms brushed.

"We have to share rooms," he said. I barely managed not to groan. "And of course we have to share with Dad and Charlotte. I don't think Dad trusts us." He slid his arm around my elbow.

I glanced down at him.

He stared back with apologetic eyes.

"I tried to get Dad to get over himself, but he wouldn't hear it. I also told him you don't sleep well when there's others in the room, but he wouldn't hear that either. I don't understand what he's so afraid of. What does he think we're going to do?"

I couldn't help but smile at that, because even I could easily find the answer to *that*. "What do you think?"

He blushed. "I *know*. I was trying not to say it, you know? It's not like we would've done it in a cabin filled with my family, even if we *were* doing it." He blushed deeper, and I turned my head down to nuzzle against the top of his head. He tilted his head back to smile up at me. "You're allowed to go back home, if you want. I won't mind. I'll come with you."

I chuckled, even though the anxiety was there, crawling just under my skin. "It'll be fine." I wasn't so sure, but I'd try my best.

I'd been doing much better lately. I was used to

Nero being around, making sounds even while asleep, and I could get a good night's sleep now with him there on the floor next to my bed.

I hadn't in the beginning, but I guess it was just a matter of getting used to it.

My bag was deposited on a double bed next to Geir's bag. The bed wasn't as big as mine, but as I was sleeping next to him it wouldn't be a problem. I'd kept my distance in the beginning, but the times he stayed over at my flat the last month before he moved, not to speak about the Autumn holiday, we'd been lying rather close. Spooning, sometimes, but also simply right next to each other, occasionally with a couple of limbs intertwined.

His family was gathered in the living room, where Daniel crouched in front of the open fireplace. He stood up the moment he saw me and came over with a big smile. "Jørgen."

We shook hands, and after him came the rest of the family. I got to meet Daniel's wife officially, as well as the daughter. Charlotte again, and her kids. The daughter wasn't so much a kid, but the son was. Yngvar came last, and though he didn't seem thrilled to see me, he shook my hand properly, smiled, and nodded.

Everyone greeted Nero as well, as he went around wagging his tail at them all.

"We're staying in tonight," Geir said as we sat down on the sofa. He scooted in close to me. "It's too late to go outside, so we decided to stay in here where it's warm and enjoy ourselves."

I draped my arm around his shoulder, too happy to be back with him back to care about the others seeing it.

The evening was actually nice.

The women played board games, and both Daniel and Yngvar joined in a couple of times. There was a crime series on the telly, a new one like they seemed to make for every Easter. There were snacks, crisps, hot chocolate.

Best of all, there was Geir.

He stayed curled up at my side all evening, and we had whispered conversations in each others' ears.

We were the first to head off to bed, leaving a napping Nero in the living room. I'd been up since six that morning, as I'd had to work before driving up the mountain to the cabin.

I suspected Geir only came with to keep me company, but I wasn't complaining. We both wore clothes to bed, T-shirts and jogging bottoms, like we always did.

"Which side do you prefer to sleep on?"

"You should sleep against the wall," I told him.

"In case I can't sleep, I don't want to disturb you if I have to get up."

He crept in first and I lay down on my back next to him.

I held out my arm, and he rolled back towards my side instantly, fitting himself to me. His head rested in the crook of my neck, and it was nice, so familiar, I instantly relaxed.

It was a shame, really, as I hadn't seen him since last October, but I fell asleep right away.

When Yngvar and Charlotte came into the room to go to bed some time later, I woke up. It was dark and they went straight to bed without making too much sound, but just knowing they were there made me tense.

Geir had moved away from me in sleep. He was on his stomach, facing away from me. Funny how that hadn't woken me up—but then I was used to his presence. Even if it had been months since the last time I'd been in it. I found his presence calming.

I lay there, trying to go back to sleep, but it wouldn't come. I was acutely aware of every sound in the room, of the smallest movement they made.

When I was sure they'd fallen asleep, I got out of bed and walked silently out of the room, into the living room. Nero was curled in front of the fire, and he lifted his head lazily as I came in. He shook his head, then put it back down on his paws again.

Lying down on the sofa, I switched the television on.

I kept the sound low so I wouldn't disturb anyone. There weren't many channels, and the nightly television programme was as crappy as ever, but it still gave me something to do besides stare at the wall.

Eventually, I fell asleep, but woke up what must have been several hours later to a freezing room. The embers in the fireplace had died out, so now the cold seeped in.

I shuffled back into the bedroom to bury myself under the duvet. Geir had moved into my place on the bed, but with a light push, he rolled over towards the wall. He didn't even so much as blink an eye.

If someone had pushed me, I would've been wide awake in seconds.

I lay there for quite a while, but I did fall asleep again—and I didn't wake until morning, when Yngvar and Charlotte got out of bed.

I was on my stomach, facing Geir, and I watched the curve of his neck and the blond tresses of his hair curl until they were both out of the room. Then I turned over onto my back and ran my hands over my face. For having been up twice in the night, I felt pretty rested.

Geir stretched, and he rolled over to fit himself against my side. He nuzzled his face against my neck. "Morning."

"Morning." I wrapped one arm around him. He was warm and hard against me.

In fact, while his body was hard and very male, there was something else entirely that was hard too, and resting against my hip.

For a moment I was afraid I'd fall right into a flashback or a panic attack, like I surely would've done last year, but... I didn't.

In fact, the strongest feeling running through me at that moment was contentment, and there was a tiny part of me that loved the fact that he was hard while pressed up against me.

It probably wasn't because of me—morning wood and all—but it still told me that he did desire me this way, because it wasn't going away.

"Does it bother you?" he muttered against the skin on my neck. He didn't move, which I was grateful for. I liked having him there, halfway atop me.

"No. Actually... not at all." In fact, my own body reacted to it.

I couldn't even remember the last time I'd reacted

like this towards anyone. Had I ever? Well, there'd been Kay… but we'd never gone that far.

I had desired him, but we'd both been too messed up to even attempt anything but friendship.

And here Geir was, all sleep-warm and cuddly and *mine*.

He was my boyfriend, he loved *me*, no matter what.

And in that moment I thought maybe I could give him everything he deserved, after all.

CHAPTER 15

*C*arina and Charlotte had set the breakfast table with every single thing one could wish for. White bread, brown bread, butter, jam, boiled eggs, fried eggs, scrambled eggs, different sorts of ham, cheese… everything a proper breakfast could ever consist of.

Everything looked good, besides the mackerel in tomato sauce and the herring, but then I'd never been very keen on fish.

After we'd eaten, Geir and I decided to head outside with Nero, and we were soon joined by all the others. We all dressed up properly so we wouldn't freeze in the Norwegian winter, and that included snowsuits, hats, scarves, and thick gloves.

Geir's cheeks were red from the cold. He was

simply adorable. He was happy and having fun, playing around in the snow with Nero. He kept making snowballs and throwing them, and Nero would be after them the moment the ball of snow left his gloved hands.

I watched them with a smile on my face, leaning back against the railing on the veranda.

"Are you doing all right?"

Daniel appeared beside me, looking at me with searching eyes.

I took my eyes off Geir to give him my attention. "Yeah."

"Good." He nodded and smiled. "I was a bit worried, I have to admit. You'd have to be around people you didn't know, and as if that wasn't enough you have to share a room. I know it's not easy for you."

"It was actually easier than expected," I admitted.

"You could sleep?" He was looking at me in that searching way again.

"Yeah. Or, well... I was up two times last night, one where I went to lie on the sofa, and once where I went back to bed. It was surprisingly easy." I kicked some snow away from my boots. "Therapy helps. And being used to Nero, that helps too."

"I'm glad, Jørgen." Daniel clapped me on the shoulder. It was the closest we ever got, though I did consider him my friend. He and Tarjei and Alex. I never got up close and personal to them either.

My personal space was reserved for only one person.

And one dog.

Geir barrelled into me then. I caught him around his waist.

"This is great!" He laughed as he leaned up to kiss my cheek. His lips, usually so warm, were freezing cold, and I shuddered. I reckoned my cheek couldn't be any better. "Isn't it great?" He leaned back to look at me, a wide smile on his face.

"It is," I said.

A few locks of hair had escaped his hat and were falling into his eyes. I brushed them away.

His smile faded a little, but his eyes lit up even more. He leaned in to kiss me again, but he didn't aim for my cheek this time. He kissed the corner of my mouth. I wanted to kiss him properly, but Daniel was right at my side and the rest of his family was scattered around us, so I settled on pulling him in closer.

His arms slid around my waist as he let himself lean on me. I glanced at Daniel and found him watching us with a small smile on his face. It widened when he caught me looking at him, and he chuckled as he walked off to leave us alone.

"Uncle likes you." Geir's head rested on my shoulder, but it was tilted back so he could look up at me. "He doesn't mind us being together at all, like Dad does."

Being reminded of him had my gaze wandering. Yngvar was across the driveway, shovelling snow that had fallen during the night. He wasn't looking our way at all.

"Dad thinks I'm too young to know what I want in life. I got him to see reason, though, that day I had the SE, and he's been a lot more positive since. He let me invite you here, too, which is awesome."

He hugged me tighter, and I returned the gesture. In part it felt good holding him and I wanted to reassure him, but also because I was reminded of that day where everything could've gone so terribly wrong for him.

My uncle had once almost died from a status epilepticus, and it tore at me to think that Geir could've as well if he hadn't got immediate medical attention. He was also lucky he'd only broken his arm and not his neck.

I knew he'd been wearing a cast for months afterward, but it was gone now. His left hand felt exactly like the right one and seemed to be functioning properly too. He'd complained once, after getting rid of the cast, that his left hand was much weaker, but I hadn't seen any evidence of it so far. I knew he'd been training it up again, which must've helped.

As for his dad... I didn't know why Yngvar didn't care for me. Maybe because I *was* six years older than his son, maybe because of my mental state, maybe because I was simply the bloke dating his son. I had no idea, but Geir and I were doing so well. I hoped, of course, that Yngvar would get over himself, but I didn't hold out hope for it.

Besides, it wasn't Geir's family I had warm feelings towards—it was just him.

"Do you want to go for a walk?" I asked, needing to get away for a bit, to be alone with him.

He nodded and we set off towards the backside of the cabin. The pine trees spread out to all sides of us, and we walked between them. They were still a dark green, and most of them were covered in snow.

"Snow's all melted back home," I said, looking upwards. "It's amazing how just driving up the mountain for a couple of hours can change the scenery so much."

His hand touched my forearm, then slid down until he tangled our gloved fingers together. "Is this okay?"

I glanced down at our entwined hands. "Of course." I'd never held hands with anyone before. It was a new feeling, having someone hold onto my hand, but I didn't mind at all. Because it was *his* hand.

We didn't walk for very long, as the snow was piled high and there was no path, so we didn't want to get lost.

But it was fifteen minutes where it was only the two of us. It was all I needed.

Before we emerged back at the cabin, I pushed him gently up against the trunk of a tree and kissed him properly, like I'd wanted to do back at the veranda. He kissed me back eagerly.

"God, I've missed you." I held him close afterwards and buried my face in the bare piece of neck visible above his scarf. He smelled good, of fresh air and soap and faintly of cologne. The past year had been hard—because he'd moved away, because I'd been alone, and because I'd had to deal with my past, which I'd only pushed away before until it unexpectedly came back to kick me in the arse.

Geir pushed my head back and up so he could rest his forehead against mine. "Two months, Jørgen. Two months, and then I'll be home."

I hadn't believed him before.

I'd been so sure he'd find someone better, find some*thing* better to do, instead of coming back to our small town and to me.

Looking into his eyes now, however, I could see

the determination, the want, the *need*, and I finally believed him.

CHARLOTTE LEFT the next day to pick up her niece and nephew at the train station.

I couldn't help but wonder where *they* were supposed to sleep. Geir didn't seem thrilled about them joining us, and when he wouldn't stop fidgeting I eventually dragged him with me to the bedroom, the only place we could currently be alone.

I stretched out on the bed and he leant back against the wall, his feet resting across my stomach. I folded my hands atop his ankles as I studied him.

"Does he still not like you, the nephew?"

He wrote about his new family in his letters, but he never said much about Charlotte's nephew. The last thing I could remember of him was *turns out he likes me after all*. Whatever that meant.

"He likes me, all right." Geir's green eyes settled on me. "It's just that… he likes me too much. A lot more than I like him."

I raised my eyebrows. "He fancies you?"

He blushed slightly but nodded. "Thing is. About what you said to me, *that* day. I—I took it to heart. We had to share a bed at Christmas, since everyone was coming down to Oslo to spend the holiday, and we kind of…" He did a vague motion with his hand.

It kind of amused me that he had a difficult time saying it. "You kind of…?"

His blush deepened.

"Well, we snogged. But that's all we ever did, and it was only that one night. I didn't want to tell you that in a letter. I wanted to tell you face to face. I don't have feelings for him, though. He's cute, obviously, but things are awkward between us, because after Christmas I kept him at a distance. I didn't want to lead him on, you know?

"The kissing itself, it didn't come natural, like it does with you. It was nice and all, but not you. My feelings are centred on you, and that's the way it'll always be." He broke off the monologue to take a breath. His eyes were guarded now as he stared at me. "I know what you said, but… Does it bother you?"

A kiss. He was acting so adorably guilty and shy for a few *kisses*.

"It doesn't." I rubbed his ankles softly. "I meant what I said. I wanted you to experience being a teenager. Teenagers experiment, that's just the way it is. I know what I said, and what it entailed, and it doesn't bother me at all. It would have if you'd gone and fancied him too, but you're here with me, so… no, it doesn't bother me at all."

He'd chosen me in the end still, and that pleased me more than anything.

He must've seen the truth in my eyes, or some other change in them, because he smiled softly and bent down to kiss me. It was a chaste kiss, just our lips brushing, but it made me want more.

More of him, more of *this* between us.

His hand cupped the back of my neck and he pulled at me, and suddenly he was flat on his back and I stretched out over him.

He spread his thighs and I lay down between them.

We kissed again, still those chaste, soft kisses. We were only wearing jogging bottoms, and as there weren't any coarse jeans in the way, I could clearly feel how he slowly got hard.

Surprisingly, my libido perked up as well, in response to feeling his desire.

He bucked up, rubbing our groins together. I groaned against his lips and ground back down against him, causing him to moan softly. He arched his back, and his arms wrapped tightly around my shoulders, digging into the coarse fabric of my knitted jumper.

Our kiss deepened as we continued to buck against

each other. I was fully hard now, which had me even more surprised, but the pleasure I felt at that moment overrode every other emotion I might've had right then.

As our speed increased, we weren't as much kissing anymore as just resting our lips against each other's. He was breathing heavily, his eyes half ways closed and glazed. He was beautiful, and it didn't do much for my self-control.

I buried my face against his neck as I came, breathing in the scent of him.

He gripped tightly at my neck as he bucked up a couple more times, then he stopped moving under me as he too gave in to his climax.

I collapsed atop him, and he hugged me close for several minutes.

When our breathing had slowed down to normal, and once his arms fell away from my shoulders, I rolled over. My shoulder connected with the wall, but I hardly noticed as I pushed myself up on my elbows and put my head in my hands.

That was the first time in my entire life where I'd willingly done anything sexual. I'd been aroused before, I had had orgasms before, but it had been my body betraying me.

My uncle always had two moods: one where all he wanted was to hurt me and get off on it, and one where he wanted *me* to get off on what he did to me. Most of the times he succeeded, with me hating myself *and* my body even more.

I knew, rationally, that it was just the body's reaction to stimulation, that it wasn't because I'd liked what he'd done to me, but I hadn't know that back then.

And now... I'd done something sexual all by my own free will, and it hadn't been bad at all. It had actually been *good*.

No, more than good.

Amazing.

My underwear wasn't feeling so comfortable at the moment, but I wouldn't take back what had happened between us for anything. It had been intimate, pleasurable, and I'd felt so *close* to him.

He wasn't a threat to me, he never had been, because all he wanted was to be with me.

All I wanted was to be with *him*.

"Jørgen." His hand landed on my shoulder, squeezing softly. "Jørgen? You're not having a flashback, are you? Or a panic attack?" He sounded worried. I hated when he was worried.

I let my forearms fall back on the bed and turned my head to look at him. "I'm fine." His eyes searched mine. I hoped he could see I spoke the absolute truth.

"I wouldn't have been if this had happened last year, but now… I'm fine."

A tentative smile spread on his lips. "You don't regret it?"

I stared at him, surprised he could even ask that. But considering my previous position, I guess I could see why he'd believe it. "No. Not at all."

I reached for him and he willingly moved into my arms. I turned on my side so I could wrap him up in my arms properly, and he pressed his face against my collarbone. He had one arm pressed between us, but the other rested over my waist.

"That was better than anything I've ever experienced," he muttered.

I chuckled. "That was better than anything I've ever experienced."

I could feel him tense up at that, but he didn't pursue the subject, for which I was grateful. I could give him a glimpse into my past from time to time, but I still wasn't able to talk about it fully without breaking down completely. Which I only did in Gina's office, where she allowed me to cry my eyes out, and she was there to bring me out of any flashback or panic attack that might happen.

I didn't even talk as freely to Daniel as I did with her. She wasn't a friend; she was just someone trained in helping me deal, and she did that wonderfully. I hadn't even had to change medication since that time I'd ended up in the hospital.

The new medication helped me function, it lowered my anxiety, and generally helped with the everyday triggers that had used to set me off before.

I still hadn't faced Jo.

I wasn't sure how I'd react when I saw him again, with or without Christina at his side. Gina and I had slowly worked our way through the abuse I'd suffered from my mother, from my uncle, how no one had seen or cared, and how my first psychiatrist had dismissed everything that had happened to me.

We were only now starting to touch upon Jo, and that might be one of the hardest things I'd ever have to deal with in therapy.

Geir squirmed against me. "I'm all sticky."

I couldn't help it, I laughed.

"Yeah. So am I."

I let him move onto his back.

He ran a hand over the front of his jogging bottoms, and my gaze zeroed in on it.

"As good as this was, I *need* to change my underwear right *now*. This is uncomfortable." He grinned at me, leaned over to kiss me one last time, then he jumped out onto the floor and started going through his bag.

I let him go to the bathroom first. I didn't feel

comfortable myself, but I still had that good, post-orgasmic feeling. I lay on my back and hooked my hands under my head, staring up at the ceiling.

Who knew I could actually be close to normal?

That I'd been able to become aroused, not to mention reach orgasm.

It was new for me, doing something like that willingly. I hadn't been forced in years, and I could finally see the difference now.

With Geir, it was because I loved him, because he was special to me.

I wanted to do anything to make him happy.

And by making him happy, I was happy too.

CHAPTER 16

*M*artin was not at all how I'd imaged he'd be.

I didn't know what it was I had imagined, I just knew it hadn't been *him*.

He was taller than Geir, but not by much, and he was too shy for words. He took one look at me and blushed bright red, not even managing to say a simple hello.

He wasn't much better with Geir, and I kept wondering how in the world Geir managed to kiss him.

"He's more confident in the dark," Geir whispered to me when I voiced the question. "He kissed *me*, believe it or not. But once the snogging was done, he was back to being the shy, awkward geek with his face buried in a book. I think it's sweet, actually, but yeah, you can see how awkward we are around each other."

Suggesting Geir enjoy his life had been a gamble.

I'd known that when I said it to him. But he was still here, only a couple of months away from a year in Oslo, and he was still with *me*. He wanted to be with me, he was attracted to me and devoted to me.

Just as I was to him.

And that was all that mattered.

That morning had proved just how attracted to him I was. I knew I should've been freaking out, that I would if it had been last year, but now I only felt a deep contentment.

I was getting better, I *could* have a normal relationship with someone, along with the intimacy that entailed.

"Does that make you the confident one?" I asked. "Because I can't see him being confident, not even in the dark."

Geir laughed and bumped his shoulder against my arm. "You sound so surprised. I should be offended."

I looked down at him. "You've changed."

Last year around this time, he'd been the shy one. The one blushing over every little thing.

Yet he was the one who'd kissed me first.

I remembered that day clearly; how happy he'd been for the necklace, which still adorned his neck, and how he'd turned his head up towards me while pulling me down the rest of the way, then the way he'd kissed me tentatively.

"For the better, I hope." He chuckled, but it came out flat. He was nervous.

I cupped the back of his neck softly, like he'd done to me over a year ago. "I can't say if it's for the better. I like you just the way you are, whether you blush for the smallest thing or if you decide to take charge. In fact, you've taken more charge than I ever have, so maybe you haven't really changed at all."

Geir mulled over what I said.

I wasn't sure it even made sense; it had tumbled out with no thought to coherency.

He smiled and stepped closer. I bent my head without being prodded and our lips brushed. It was only that brief kiss, as we were still in the living room with everyone else, but it was enough.

"Two months," he whispered, his eyes closed.

Two more months until he would finally come home. Two months until we wouldn't have to be apart anymore and meet for only a week during his school holidays.

Only two more months and I could be with him every single day.

His eyes opened and they were such a brilliant green that they startled me for a moment.

"Two months," I said, running my hand over his cheek in a caress.

～

THAT EVENING, when everyone settled down around the table playing board games or watching crime shows on the telly, Geir and I took Nero outside.

We stood on the veranda while Nero went running right out into the deepest of the snow piles.

I wrapped my arms around Geir's shoulder and rested my cheek against the top of his head.

He leaned back against me, his gloved hands gripping my forearms. "What happens when I come back home?"

"What do you mean? We'll be together."

"Properly?"

"Aren't we already properly together?"

"Yes. Kind of. You gave me permission to do whatever I wanted this year. But when I come home... We'll be exclusive, right?"

"If that's what you want." That was what I wanted. I might be okay with him living his teenage life in Oslo, but I didn't think I could handle it when he moved back.

"It is." He tilted his head slightly so his nose brushed the skin above my scarf. He was cold, and the contact made me jerk a bit in surprise, but I only tightened my arms around his shoulders. "What about everything else, though?"

"I'm not following. What else is there? We'll be exclusive. Just you and me."

"What about the living situation? I still don't know what I want to do with my life, so I have to find a job. I don't know how easy that's going to be, with my epilepsy and all."

"Employers aren't allowed to pass you over simply because of your condition. If you're qualified for the job, and no one else has better qualifications, they're bound to hire you." I didn't think him finding a job would be difficult. Depended on what he wanted to do, of course, but he was talented. He'd find something. "As for the living situation... I was hoping, I guess, that when you came back, you came back to me. Like, properly."

He tensed a bit in my arms. "You mean... living together?"

I nodded.

Being without him for a year had brought home the fact that I wanted him with me at all times. We'd spent almost every evening together before he moved, and though we hardly ever spent the night together, I wanted that too now.

I was ready for it.

I could sleep with someone else in the room now, especially if that someone was him.

"I would love that," he whispered, and I could feel his body relax.

I knew it would be hard getting used to have someone around all the time, but once he came back I didn't want to let him go. Ever. I wanted him with me, in my home.

Just us two, together.

And Nero too, of course.

"What if I can't get a job?"

I glanced down to see him biting down on his lower lip. "You will. It might not happen right away, but we'll make do. I've got a job, I'm making money, and I don't really have much to spend it on. It won't be a problem."

"Are you sure?"

I couldn't stand not looking at him, so I turned him around, sliding my arms down around his back instead of around his shoulder. "I am sure. Couldn't be surer."

He put his arms up between us, pressed up against both our chests. "I don't want to live off you. It's been fine with Dad, because I've been underage and all that. But I'm eighteen now, and when school's over I want to make my own way."

"And you will. You'll find a job. You'll figure out what you want to do. But you shouldn't jump into anything before you're certain, either."

He should like whatever job he ended up with, or else he'd be miserable.

He stared up at me.

"I love you." It came out almost as a sigh, and I could tell from the way his eyes widened that he hadn't meant to say it.

I put my forehead down to rest against his.

If I'd learned anything the past year, it was how deep my feelings for him ran. That I loved him more than anything else.

And he needed to know that.

Just as he hadn't wanted to tell me about Martin in a letter, I hadn't wanted to tell him over the phone.

Standing outside in the cold, brisk winter evening surrounded by snow and darkness… it reminded me of our first kiss, in front of his house that night over a year ago.

It was the perfect setting.

"I love you too."

He smiled widely, nose rubbing gently against mine. He cupped one palm around my cheek, thumb stroking my skin lovingly.

"Thank you."

"For what?"

"For saying those words." He brushed a feather-light kiss over my lips. His lips were cold—but so were mine.

"I mean them." I'd never meant anything more in my entire life.

He couldn't stop smiling. "You have no idea how happy it makes me."

If it made him as happy as I felt right now, I had a clue. "All I want is for you to be happy."

"Oh, I am. Never been happier." He brushed his lips against mine again, a little harder this time. "There's only one thing that can make me happier right now, and that's if it was already June. If school was already over and I could go back home with you."

"Soon." Two months weren't long. It was nothing at all compared to the last ten months we'd spent apart.

"Living together," he whispered, pressing up closer to me. "Are you sure you're ready for that?"

"I am."

"You can't stay awake every night. Or sleep on the sofa."

"I know."

Geir was quieter in sleep than Nero. Nero kept

getting up to change positions, he had dreams that made him growl or jerk in his sleep. Considering we shared a bed most nights, Geir would be nothing in comparison.

His gaze searched mine. What it searched for, I didn't know.

"I never imagined we'd get here," he said then. "I hoped, of course, but that we've come so far… it's incredible. We live so far away from each other, but we're still together. And in only two months, we'll *truly* be together again. It's incredible."

"That it is." I was incredibly lucky to have him in my life.

If he hadn't had is seizure in front of my flat that day, I probably never would've met him. Or at least not got to know him.

I had all of this because of that day, that small incident.

If it weren't for him, and his presence in my life, I might've continued on like I had. Not getting close to anyone, going to work, going home, struggle to sleep, and do it all over again. Day after day.

Now, after meeting him, I was back in therapy. I was confronting my past. I was getting *better*.

I'd had my first sexual encounter that wasn't forced upon me—and that was the most incredible of all.

"Don't fret about getting a job," I said, voice low. "Focus on your exams, of finishing school. Come back. Come live with me. When *that's* done, then you can start looking for jobs. But don't settle for anything but what feels right. We'll make it, no matter what. My job pays well, the flat's paid off. I'm in a good place economically. All I want is for you to be with me, and for you to be happy there."

"As long as I have you, I'll be happy." He moved his head so our cheeks slid together. His was smooth, while mine had some stubble that rasped against his skin.

"The same goes for me." I pulled him into a tight hug. "I'd do anything for you, Geir. *Anything*."

He drew in a breath, then nuzzled against my neck as he let it out. "I can't wait till the end of June."

"Me neither." I rested my cheek against his head and stared out at Nero, who still entertained himself in the snow. He currently rolled over in one of the piles Yngvar had made when he shovelled the driveway earlier.

The front door opened.

"There you are." Charlotte stuck her head out to smile at us. "Supper's ready."

We unentangled ourselves.

"We'll be in in a minute," Geir said as he turned to face her.

"Don't take too long, or else there won't be any left for you," she teased, but withdrew and closed the door after her.

"You okay?" Geir took my hand and squeezed.

"Yeah." I looked into his worried eyes. "I'm great, actually."

A smile spread slowly on his lips. "That's good."

I kissed him once more, then whistled for Nero as we moved towards the door. Nero's ears perked up and he turned his head, and when I held the door open to him he came pelting up on the veranda.

In the hall, he shook all his snow off—spraying us with it.

Geir laughed. "Charo used to do that when he was younger. He *loved* snow."

I grabbed Nero's collar before he could venture further into the cabin and rubbed the wet snow off him with the towel that lay ready just for these occasions.

"Do you want a new dog?" I asked him, upon seeing the way he gazed down at Nero.

He nodded. "I do. But not yet. When I'm settled back home, with you, and with Nero, maybe. We'll see."

Once I let Nero go, he ran ahead of us into the living room.

I stayed back and drew Geir into a one-armed

hug. "Whenever you're ready. I reckon Nero'd like to get a friend to play with. Two dogs have company in each other when we're not home, right?"

He leant against me. "Yeah. I'm starting to feel ready for it, another dog. But I don't want another Labrador—nor another seizure response dog. I want a dog who can just be a dog, you know? Who doesn't have to take care of me. I can take care of myself."

That he could.

And whatever he wanted, he'd get. I'd make sure of it.

CHAPTER 17

*N*ero jumped on me the moment I entered the door, causing me to nearly drop the mail I held in one hand.

I pushed him down sternly. He knew he wasn't allowed to jump on people, not even me.

When he sat at my feet, tail wagging, I finally patted his head.

I threw the mail on the coffee table on my way into the bedroom to change. What I really wanted to put on was my comfy jogging bottoms, but I had to go for a walk with Nero, so I changed from work clothes to my Gore-Tex trousers, as well as a new T-shirt and a thick jumper. It rained outside, so I'd also have to wear my Gore-Tex jacket as well.

Nero's tail started wagging in more excitement as

he saw my clothes. These clothes always meant that we were going out.

I grabbed my mail again to sort through it.

I kept hold of the ad papers so I could throw them away on my way out, and tossed the bills on the table. There was a letter there too, and my heart practically jumped up in my throat, as it did *every* time.

I'd got many letters from Geir in the past eleven months, and yet I still felt a mix of excitement and nervousness every time I received a new one. I kept them all too, in a box stashed in the bottommost shelf in my closet.

As much as I wanted to read the letter right now, Nero wasn't having any of it. He butted his head against me, and when I looked down at him he ran towards the door.

"All right, all right." I sighed and sat the letter down on the coffee table. I laced up my waterproof boots, zipped up my jacket, and put the harness over Nero's head, fastening it around his back.

As soon as I clipped the leash to the harness, we were ready to go, as evidenced by Nero's excited pull on it.

I stepped back in surprise once I opened the door, however, because on my doorstep stood Jo. His hand was raised slightly, like he'd been about to knock. Which was probably the case.

I stared at him, taken aback at finding myself face to face with him so suddenly.

He seemed to be just as surprised, because he stared back at me for a moment before he managed to regain control of himself.

"Um, hey." He took a step back, away from me, and bowed his head.

Nero pulled more on the leash, longing to get out and do his business, but I held him tight.

"What're you doing here?" It had been over a year since last I saw him. The last time had been at the shop, the first time Geir had seen me right in the middle of a flashback and a panic attack. I didn't feel either was forthcoming at the moment, but having him there made me extremely uncomfortable.

"I wanted to talk to you." Jo looked up at me again, but I couldn't decipher his expression.

What could he possibly have to talk to me about?

"I have to take Nero out for a walk."

"I'll walk with you."

"It's raining."

He shrugged. "It's just water."

So that was how I found myself walking the trail up by the graveyard with my estranged brother.

I unclipped Nero's leash as soon as we were up on the trail, and he set off ahead of us, leaving me behind with Jo. I immediately regretted letting him go as I watched his tail wag as he sniffed around, because while he'd been leashed I could focus all my attention on him.

Now I actually had to focus on Jo, who hadn't said a word as we'd walked up to the graveyard and through it.

"Christina told me you have a boyfriend," he said.

"How does she know about that?"

"I don't know. She didn't say." Jo shrugged. "I am —I'm happy for you. That you can—uh, I mean, that you're able to—" He ran a frustrated hand through his hair, which was already soaking wet from the rain.

"Be normal?" I suggested.

"I guess, yeah." He buried his hands in his jeans pockets now and hunched his shoulders. He looked lost, like he didn't know what else to say or do.

Christina's words from that first day I'd stayed over at Thomas' house rang loud and clear in my head. *Jo loves you, you know that, right? He has his reasons, you know. Maybe you should hear them before you make up your mind about him.*

I'd been thinking about those words a lot, about the meaning behind them, but I hadn't managed to reach a conclusion. Truth of the matter was that Jo hadn't been through the same as I'd been.

That I knew.

"Christina said—"

"Jørgen, I—"

We both shut up and glanced awkwardly at each other.

I didn't think I'd ever had a proper conversation with Jo. My childhood had been hell, while he'd kept away from it all. Even when he was home, he hadn't been put through the same things I'd been.

He'd been the favourite.

I didn't know what that made me.

Mum hadn't liked me at all, Dad hadn't given a shit, and my uncle… He'd liked me too much.

"You go first." Jo nodded to me, but he didn't meet my gaze.

I didn't even know what I'd been about to say. Not really. "Christina said you had your reasons. I don't really know what she meant by that, but yeah. She said it." I stared down at my feet. The gravel was wet and muddy, and I would have to wash my shoes when I got home. Or maybe wait for all the mud to dry first, then wash them after it had flaked off.

I could see him fidget in the corner of my eye. "You are the biggest victim of our childhood, Jørgen. I know that. Everybody knows that. What you had to go through… no one should have to go through that. I just… It wasn't easy for me either."

"How could you have suffered?" I turned to him, anger flaring. "He didn't come into your bed at night. You weren't the one locked up in the dark, not knowing when you would be let out or when you would get to eat next."

"I know, Jørgen! I know all of that. Don't you think I wanted to help you? That I wanted to do something for you? I hated not being able to be of any help."

"You could've gone to the police long before you actually did."

That would've been the best help he could've given. Maybe I could've been free of the abusive a few years earlier, if only he had done something.

He took a shaky breath. "I was a kid too, Jørgen. I wanted to help my little brother; that was all I wanted to do. But you know what I was told? I was told if I did anything, if I told *anyone*, you would die. I didn't want my little brother to die! So I was left to watch everything that happened and not being able to do anything about it. Being told something like that all my life... What was I supposed to do?"

I didn't have an answer to that. I kept staring at my shoes as the trail started sloping downwards.

"When you tried to kill yourself... Tarjei rang me after he found you, you know. He cried and he yelled, and I knew that as long as you were in hospital they couldn't do anything to you. So I went to the police. I went and told them everything." He took a breath. "I know I should've done something sooner, but having been told that when I was a kid… I had no idea if they would kill you or not. They were both capable of it. I just wanted my little brother to live."

I looked at him. There were raindrops on his face.

He wiped them away once he realised I'd seen them, and he refused to meet my eyes.

No, not raindrops. Tears.

"I don't know what else I was supposed to do." He sounded *wrecked*. "Uncle was a sadistic bastard. So was she." He took a shaky breath. "You know, he suffered a status epilepticus once, when I was in the room with him. I just stood there. I wanted him to die *so much*. But Mum came in and realised what was going on. I've never experienced such a beating in my life as I got then. I know that isn't anything to what you went through, but still. If she hadn't come in, I would've let him rot there."

Jo would've let him die.

He would've done that—for me.

It felt like I was going to choke. My chest felt as though it was being squeezed, and my body trembled.

I dropped Nero's leash and grabbed at the collar

of my jacket and jumper, pulling them both down and away from my throat. It didn't help one bit, and I bent over.

"Jørgen!"

I cupped my hands in front of my mouth and nose and tried to take deep, slow breaths. I knew that slowing my breathing would ease the symptoms, but doing it without someone else around to ease me out of it was a lot more difficult. I breathed in deeply through my nose and slowly out again through my mouth.

Calm, calm, calm.

Be calm.

The choking sensation slowly ebbed away, as did the chest pain. My breathing gradually calmed.

I removed my hands from my face and straightened up once I'd gathered the leash from the ground.

Nero stood in front of me, head cocked curiously. He was held back by Jo, who looked alarmed and worried and completely lost as to what to do.

"You can let him go," I croaked out, nodding my head towards Nero.

Jo did, and Nero came running up to me. He was soaking wet from the rain, but so was I, so I didn't give a damn when he jumped up on me. I hugged him tight and let him lick my cheek.

"Are you all right?" Jo sounded like he didn't know if he was allowed to ask that question.

I nodded. "I'm fine."

I was tired despite my words. A panic attack always took my energy, even if I managed to nip it before it had got worse.

And it could've got a *lot* worse; I knew that all too well.

"We should head back." I couldn't take the long way around today. All I wanted right then was to go back home and collapse on the sofa.

Jo didn't protest, so we headed back.

Nero ran ahead of us again, and Jo came up to walk at my side.

We walked in silence for a while. The rain continued, and though I was wearing Gore-Tex all over, I was cold and wet, as well as exhausted from bringing myself back from the panic attack.

"I'm sorry, Jørgen. I shouldn't have brought it up."

I glanced at him. He was the one staring at his feet now.

"It's okay," I muttered.

"I hate that we're not talking. You're my little brother. I just— I don't know how to talk to you. It's all my fault, because I never talked to you when we grew up either, but it was easier for me to just stay away. I know it wasn't easy for you, and it doesn't excuse it at all, but... I just want us to be brothers, you know?"

I didn't know, but I nodded once anyway.

Our childhood had been so far from what most other people experienced. It had been hell for me, and looking back now, I knew it couldn't have been easy for him either.

But knowing it and accepting it were two different matters altogether. I didn't know if I could put all those years behind me, but at the same time... he *was* my brother.

I'd become closer to the extensive family ever since my stay at Thomas' house. That didn't mean I could be around them for hours at a time, but I visited more often than I had before.

Alex was the one I was closest to—and he wasn't even family.

Still, Jo was the only one of my closest family I could ever imagine having a relationship with.

"I understand if you think it's too difficult," he said as we started down towards the graveyard. "I should've done something sooner. I should've been there for you during the trial and afterwards. I just couldn't face you... and I was sectioned, so— Anyway, Christina's been on me for years about mending things with you, but I never could get myself to do it. I was too afraid. I'm still afraid, because I know I don't *deserve* mending things with you."

Wasn't I afraid to face him too? We were both victims of our childhood, but in quite different ways.

It was time I came with my confession.

"I can't stand being around you and Christina because you're cousins and you're together, and it's not so far from cousins to uncle and nephew."

CHAPTER 18

*H*e stopped dead, face pale.

"Oh shit. I—I haven't even thought of that. Shit." He bowed his head. "It's—Christina and I, we're the real deal. I want to be with her. I know she's our cousin, and some people think it's weird and even disgusting, but the truth of the matter is that it's not illegal. I am allowed to marry her, if I want to. Whereas what happened to you... that is illegal in so many ways."

"I know it's different. I just wanted to get it out there. It makes me uncomfortable." I clenched my hands, one into a fist and the other around Nero's leash. "She doesn't make me uncomfortable on her own, but you two together does. You make me uncomfortable." I knew that hurt him to hear, but it was the truth.

We were down in the graveyard now, and I whistled for Nero. He came running back to me and stood quietly as I clipped the leash back on his harness. He'd been well-trained when I'd got him, and though I hadn't done much in the way of training, he'd stuck to what he'd learned from his old owners.

Something teased at the back of my mind. Something he'd said earlier, but I couldn't quite grasp it.

"I wish we could try," Jo said after a long moment of silence.

"Try what?"

"To be brothers."

I didn't answer, because I didn't know what to say.

On one hand, I would like that too, a little bit.

On the other hand, it was all so very painful. There was so much bitterness on my part, directed towards him.

I didn't know if I could get over that.

"I'm happy for you," he said. "About the boyfriend, I mean."

I had to clear my throat before replying. "Thanks."

"I'm glad that you're able to—to have a relationship, after everything."

"It's thanks to therapy and medication," I muttered. I reined Nero in as a car came towards us. We were on the pavement, but he was still a young dog and cars were exciting.

"Christina told me about—" It was his turn to clear his voice. "About the hospitalisation last July. I wanted to go visit you, but... I was scared. Like I've been all these years. It reminded me too much of *that* time, when I realised I *had* to go the police. If it didn't stop, you'd try to kill yourself again and you would've probably succeeded. I am so sorry I didn't go to them before, but I was so bloody *scared*."

My chest squeezed again. "Can we not talk about that? Please? Just—Don't talk about it. It's in the past, it can't be undone or changed." I had enough of the past in therapy, I didn't want to think about it when I wasn't there anymore. I was doing better, and I didn't want to jeopardise that by going back over everything.

"I can't promise we'll be close, Jo, but I can try. I mean, there's a lot of bitterness. I used to *hate* you. But I can work on that. I know it wasn't easy for you either. Gina's been on me about you, for a while. Maybe—maybe we could go see her together." That was all I could offer for now.

"Gina?" He cast a confused look at me.

"My psychiatrist." I stared back, challenging.

"Right." He looked away.

"Maybe you should see someone professional too." It had sure helped me, even if it was the hardest thing I'd ever done. Living through what I had was one thing, but having to relive everything again in sessions with her... I hated it. But I knew I was doing better, so in the end I guess it was all worth it.

"I am seeing someone. Have for years."

And that's when it clicked, what nagged at me, what he'd said earlier. *Sectioned*. "You were sectioned?"

He swallowed audibly. "Yeah."

"What for?" What could possibly have landed him in hospital? And against his own free will, even.

"Because I'm—" He licked his lips nervously, unable to so much as look my way. "Because I was manic. In a psychosis. I was a danger to myself and others. So they sectioned me—and now I've got a diagnosis. I'm bipolar. Bipolar I, the most severe form."

Bipolar... Manic depression. I didn't know much about it, but I knew the gist of it.

"I've got more manic episodes than depressive ones," Jo said in a low voice. "But they're both pretty bad. When I'm depressed, nothing matters, because I'm so far down in a black hole there's no way up. All I want is to die. And when I'm manic, nothing matters either, because I'm either so happy that everything else falls to the wayside or I'm so irritable all I want is for everyone else to bugger off. Or if I'm psychotic... well. Then I'm not in touch with reality at all."

That didn't sound any fun at all.

"I was like that growing up. Spiralling from one extreme to the other, and no one gave a shit. You might think I was the favourite, but I wasn't, Jo. I was mentally ill and not a single person bothered to get me help for it. Like no one bothered to help you." He glanced at me briefly, but now I was the one who couldn't meet his gaze.

What Jo was telling me... it painted a totally different version of our childhood. For him, anyway, mine was still the same. Mine would never change. But I'd always thought Jo was loved, that he'd never been hurt.

"When I was in a normal mood, on my baseline, all I wanted was to help you. But when I spiralled, either into a depression or into mania, it didn't matter. Either I couldn't do anything, because I was too depressed, or nothing mattered because every-thing in my life was so *fast*. And then there were times when I wanted our uncle to die, like that time he had an SE."

He ran a hand through his wet hair. "I don't know

if I was on my baseline then or if I was irritable or depressed or what... All I remember is an all-consuming need for him to rot in hell. And I hate that Mum came in, that she helped him."

"I wish he would've died that day," I whispered. "I'm glad he blew his brains out eventually. I wish *she'd* died too." I had no love for them, absolutely no love. They'd never done anything but hurt me, and if I'd ever had any feelings for them but hate at all, they were long dead.

We continued on in silence.

"Are you okay now?" I asked after a while. "Not manic or depressed, I mean."

"I'm on medications that keeps it mostly in check. I have episodes now and then, but not as full-blown as they used to be." Jo shook his head, splashing water everywhere. Not that it mattered, as it still rained. "I'm on anti-depressants, mood stabilisers, anti-psychotics, the whole shebang. It makes life easier."

"Yeah." Medication did that for me too. I supposed I was mentally ill too, PTSD was a mental disorder, after all. But I could get better from it. I could get healthy again—not that I thought I would, my issues ran too deep, but people got better from PTSD.

As for bipolar... That was chronic, wasn't it?

"So Christina knows?" She was the one who'd said he had his reasons. Had she meant only the fact they'd threatened me to keep him silent? Or did she also know about his mental state?

"Oh, she knows. She knows everything." His voice was vehement, which made me think she knew a lot more about him than I ever would. "Christina and I first hooked up in her last year of secondary, during her *russ* celebrations. I was back in town, supposed to be on medication after my stay in hospital, but I didn't take them. First time we were intimate, I was so manic."

He stared ahead of us, but he had a faraway look in his eyes that told me he wasn't quite in the here-and-now.

"She realised something was wrong, eventually. When I became more erratic, took dangerous risks. When I went into a psychosis... I don't really remember that part. I got sectioned again, anyway. Next time I came out of hospital, I continued taking my medication. I fixed things with Christina, and we... we've been together since."

So much I never knew. How had this escaped me for most of my life? Had I never noticed Jo acting weirdly? That his mood fluctuated from one extreme to another?

The sad thing was that the answer to those questions were a sound *no*. I'd never noticed anything, because Jo and I had never been close. I'd been too wrapped up in my misery, while he'd been dealing with his own hell.

"I'm not telling you this as an excuse, Jørgen."

I blinked at him.

"Because it's not. But aside from being afraid they'd hurt you—*kill you*—I wasn't always in a right mind. In fact, I spent most of my teenaged years ill, either up or down. I wasn't often on baseline, I kept cycling from manic to depressed and back again. And each episode lasted *months*."

How come the school hadn't noticed? It was what I wanted to ask him, but I knew the answer. It was the same as it was for me. Why hadn't the school ever noticed something was wrong with me?

I hadn't had friends—except the one. I never talked in class. I never participated. I wouldn't let anyone touch me. I had panic attacks even back then. Yet every single adult at the school had turned a blind eye.

"I'm not sure," I eventually said, when the silence stretched out.

"Not sure about what?"

"If I *can*. Have a relationship with you." I wiped raindrops away from my eyes. "I don't know. All these years…"

He sighed. "I understand."

"Maybe. But I don't—I don't know." Part of me wanted to, part of me revolted at the simple thought.

"It's okay. I didn't expect this to lead anywhere." He huddled in his jacket. "I just needed to get all the cards on the table. I took the first step, and now—the ball's in your court now, Jørgen. Whatever you decide, I'll go along with. Even if it is nothing at all."

My chest squeezed tight, like it did right before a panic attack, except this time it didn't lead to one. "Okay." It was all I could say.

He nodded. Only once, but it was a confirmation, an agreement.

We parted ways after that. He was drenched to the skin, and I wasn't much better.

My shoes and trousers kept my lower part dry, but rain had snuck down the collar of my jacket, wetting my jumper and T-shirt.

I stripped once I entered my flat, then brought Nero with me into the bathroom. I washed him, dried him up, then jumped in to the shower myself.

Once I was done and finally dressed in my comfy joggers, I went back into the living room to pick up Geir's letter.

I looked at it, turned it around in my fingers, weight it.

It was a white envelope with my name written

elegantly on the front, like usual. He always wrote to me about everyday things. Things we didn't talk about on the phone. How his days had been. It was all cheerful and normal, unless he was angry at his dad, then he could ramble on for a few paragraphs.

I bit my lip as I looked down at my name. I'd never written him back, not once. For the letter I'd received before Christmas, he'd said that his wish was to get a letter back. I didn't have anything to say; all those everyday things that he wrote about didn't happen in my life.

Sure, I met up with Tarjei or Alex, but that was about it. I didn't have family to write about or school or classmates. My job as the same boring stuff everyday that I was sure he didn't want to hear about.

At the same time, it was very difficult for me to talk to him about everything that bothered me.

Where his letters were trivial—never mentioning anything traumatic, because he'd never experienced anything bad, except Charo's death and I'd been there for that—maybe I could write a letter to him about everything I couldn't say aloud?

He was the most important person in my life.

He deserved to know.

I took the letter with me into the second bedroom, which functioned as my office. There was only a desk, my laptop, and bookcases in there. There was nothing personal about that room—it was cool and unwelcoming.

It also had a door.

I hated doors, which was why the rest of the flat was very open.

I sat down at the desk, pulled up a notebook, and found a black pen.

Then I started to write.

PART V
HOW LONG SINCE THIS STORY BEGAN

GEIR

CHAPTER 19

Geir,

I appreciate all the letters you've sent me over the past year. They mean a lot to me, but I'm not much of a writer myself. That is why this is the only letter you'll ever receive from me. The only reason I'm writing it is because I want to tell you everything, and I can't say it to you face to face. You deserve to know, but I don't ever want to talk about it. I can't. I do in therapy, and that takes everything out of me. So, I figured, where you write me trivial, light letters, I'll write one telling you about everything that's ever happened to me.

I can't remember a time where I wasn't a victim of abuse. Maybe it started the moment I was born. I honestly don't know, and I don't think I want to know.

What I do know though, is that my family has never even been close to normal. My dad was absent, always working, never home to take care of his wife and kids. He left that to my mum's brother, and I bet you've already guessed that he didn't do a very good job of taking care of us.

My mum is sick. She's always been sick. She suffers from what's now called dissociative identity disorder. Throughout my childhood, it was known as multiple personalities. And she had them in spades. I wonder sometimes what happened to her to break her like that, but other times I just wish she'd rot in hell. She was never nice, never caring. She yelled, she pushed, she shoved, she slapped, and she hit us. Especially me. Her favourite pastime was to lock me in the basement, in total darkness, with me not knowing when I'd get out or when I'd get to eat, or what was even down there because there wasn't any light.

I hate dark, locked rooms. That's why I prefer to sleep with the light on, even if my bedroom doesn't have a door. I removed that the moment I moved into my flat. I hate her for what she's done to me. The fact that she's mentally ill doesn't matter, nor does the fact that she must've been through worse to become like that. I just... I hate her.

Then there was her brother. My uncle. I can't remember a time when he wasn't around, when he wasn't creeping into my room at night. I don't even know how old I was that first time, just that I can't remember it ever being any different. He was always there at night. I'm not going to give you the details, because I don't think I could even write them down for you. Gina is the only one who knows everything, not because I trust her more than you, but because she's an outsider. Because it's her job.

Suffice to say, he was mostly cruel. It was all about him and his pleasure. He was sadistic. But there were sometimes when he would be all about me, and I hate to think about those times even more. I was so ashamed of myself. Still am, to a degree, though I'm coming to terms with it. It's difficult to reverse the thinking patterns I've had since I was a child, though.

He's the one who had epilepsy, which is why I know so much about it. I had to take care of him when my mum wasn't around. Jo told me, not long ago, that he'd contemplated letting him lie there during an SE, hoping he'd die from it. Does it make me a bad person that I wish he had? He would've, you know, if Mum hadn't been there. When he told me that, I had a panic attack. I never thought Jo cared about me or did anything for me. Turns out he does care, and he was as much a victim as I was without going through the same treatment as me.

I tried to kill myself when I was fifteen. That's the scars on my forearms. Jo went to the police after that, and though I've known that he was the one who told them, I still couldn't stand to be around him. I wonder if I'd been more forgiving towards him when I was younger if I'd known what he'd been told. They'd said to him, when he was just a kid too, that if he ever told anyone, they'd kill me. And he didn't want me to die.

I didn't know about this until last month. He approached me and we had a chat. I have so much bitterness towards him, but that chat… I appreciated it. I wish… I don't know what I wish. For him to be a proper brother, maybe? For us to be close? They're one and the same, I guess. I want to try and forgive him, but I'm not sure I can. There's so many years of hate and bitterness on my part, because I always saw him getting off easy while I had to deal with our mother's rage and our uncle's advances. Still, Jo's sick too, and our childhood wasn't easy for him either.

I don't like using those words about them. Mum and Uncle… they were never the definition of those words. Vanja and Erlend, that's their names. I can't stand to use them either though.

He put a gun to his head after being questioned by the police. I'm glad he's gone, but I wish he could've lived to get what he deserved. But then again, maximum prison sentence is only twenty-one years, so eventually he would've been out on the streets again. This way, he's gone forever.

She's locked up in a mental facility, where I hope they'll keep her until she kicks the bucket. I don't ever want to see her face again. Dad went to prison for a couple of years, and he was sentenced to pay a good sum of money in compensation. It was one of the most brutal child abuse cases that had ever come forth back then. He's out now though, been out for a while, but I haven't seen or spoken to him. As far as I know, he's dead. He's moved away from town, so there's not a single chance of ever meeting him by accident. Good riddance.

This wasn't the end, as much as I'd wished it would be. I guess I must've had victim tattooed on my forehead back then, because my gym teacher kept me back one day. I was never part of gym, so I reckoned he wanted to talk about that. He didn't. It was only that once, but you can guess what happened.

After Jo went to the police, I was sent to see a psychiatrist. It was a middle-aged man and he didn't believe me. Or maybe he did, but he didn't have any compassion. Maybe, inside, he was like them. He told me to get over myself. I never went back to therapy.

I lived with my grandma until I turned eighteen. This was before she moved to Spain, where she's still living. She left me well enough alone. Maybe she sensed that I needed space, maybe she didn't know how to deal with me... I don't know. When I was eighteen and *graduated school, when I got my apprenticeship, I moved into my own flat. I've lived by myself ever since.*

I know when you said the only thing you wished for Christmas was a letter in return, you didn't mean this kind of letter. I know it's long and utterly depressing, but I want you to know everything. If you haven't already guessed it, that is. Still, this will fill out what you already know.

I don't ever want to talk about this, so I beg you not to ever bring it up. Unless I bring it up myself, this is something I want to lie dead. I just wanted you to know, so you know what you're getting yourself into with me. So you know exactly what I've been through. Everything related to this is triggering for me, though not as much as it used to be back before you moved.

Therapy has helped a lot. I'm doing much better. But all this history is there, and I still don't know how to deal with it effectively. I don't know how to deal with Jo, or his relationship with Christina. They're still cousins and that still upsets me, even though I know it's not illegal, I know they're grown up and willing.

I'm sorry for pushing all of this on you. It was just this once. I won't ever do it again.

Jørgen

J wiped my eyes and folded the papers back together. I cried just as much now as the first twenty times I'd read the letter. It was a thick bunch of papers, longer than any letter I'd ever written to him. Two, if not three times as long.

I might've guessed about his uncle, but I hadn't even imagined it could've been as bad as the truth was.

Charlotte walked into the room. "Geir, do you want to—Why are you crying? Geir?"

I dropped the letter on my lap and wiped more thoroughly at my eyes.

"Is something wrong?"

"It's nothing." I desperately tried to wipe all the tears away. "What do you want?"

She frowned, then came to sit on the coffee table in front of me. "We've been here since last evening. Why haven't you gone to see Jørgen yet?"

And just like that, she'd got right down to the heart of the matter.

Because, truth was, I could've gone straight to Jørgen's last night, and I hadn't. I'd gone back home with Dad and Charlotte, to my aunt and uncle's place.

"We haven't talked on the phone in over two weeks because I've been so busy with exams. What if he's changed his mind in that time?" It was silly, I knew it deep down, yet the fear was still there.

"Geir." Charlotte sighed and gave me a look that told me exactly how idiotic I was being. "You really think he's gone and changed his mind?"

"Yes. No. I don't know." My foot bounced nervously.

"Now, I don't know Jørgen well. But after Easter, at the cabin… There is no doubt that he's fully dedicated to you. I mean, he came there, clearly uncomfortable, just to be with you. Because your dad was being unreasonable, you even had to share a room with us, and yet he stayed. He stayed the whole week, and it wasn't for anyone else but you. Just from seeing him that week, I highly doubt he'd ever change his mind about you."

"I know. I know that." I closed my eyes. "God, it's so silly. I'm finally here, what I've been waiting for for a year, and I can't bring myself to go over there and face him. Just because of some childish fear. I know, rationally, that I don't have to worry. I know he'll be happy to see me."

Charlotte sat up straighter. "Come for a walk with me and your dad. Maybe that'll set your head straight again."

I chuckled and slid the folded papers back into the envelope, ran upstairs to put it in my suitcase, then I went back downstairs. They were already dressed, but all I had to do was step into my beat-up Converse.

Dad threw me curious glances every other minute as we headed towards the graveyard.

I tried ignoring him, but Charlotte wasn't so tactical.

"He's being an idiot," she said. "He's scared."

"I am *not* scared." I was, though. Now that I was back home, it was the real deal. What if he'd changed his mind about us, or me moving in with him? I should've called him, but I'd been so busy with exams and then I'd been busy packing so I could finally go home.

But now that I was here, I was too chicken to show up at his door.

Dad and Charlotte walked a different route than the one I used to take. They walked down the entire graveyard, and took my usual route the other way around. There were upwards slopes than the other way, where it all went downhill.

Dad and Charlotte held hands. I noticed on our way up the worst of the slopes, when I lagged a bit behind. Their fingers were casually linked, and something suddenly hit me straight in the chest. Longing, anticipation… I wasn't sure. All I knew was that it felt uncomfortable, like something was pressing against my chest from the inside.

We reached the top of the slope, and I wondered what it would be like to walk casually like that with Jørgen, when I *saw* him.

He wasn't on the path, instead standing in a small clearing off it. He looked out at the sea, but I knew his profile anywhere.

I couldn't see Nero, but I knew he had to be around somewhere too.

I stopped walking so I could stare at him.

He looked exactly the same. He wore his loose-fitting hiking trousers, but on his upper body he only had on a tight-fitting vest, which showed off more skin than I'd ever seen him show. It seemed almost golden in the sunlight and his tattoo stood out starkly against it. His short white-blond hair was spiked up.

All in all, he looked amazing.

I pushed past Dad and Charlotte, who hadn't even noticed I'd stopped.

He must've heard me coming, because he turned around. His gaze settled on me, and his eyes widened in surprise.

I launched myself at him, and he caught me easily up in his arms.

Nero came shooting out from behind a tree at just

that moment, right at Jørgen's legs, and we tumbled to the ground.

I landed on top, so only my knees made contact with the ground, which thankfully was covered in heather and grass.

Jørgen, on the other hand, had the breath knocked out of him, but he regained it quickly. I leaned down to kiss him once before I removed myself so he could get back up.

"Are you all right?" he asked me.

I nodded with a smile. "The big question here is if you are?" I walked close to brush heather and grass and pine needles off his back.

His arms slid around my waist and I leaned against him. "I am."

I grinned up at him.

"Hi. I'm home."

"Yeah, I can see that." He smiled back, a wide smile showing teeth. "Welcome home."

He kissed me.

The brief kiss I'd given him when we were on the ground had been nothing. This was the kiss I'd wanted, the one I'd been longing for. There was nothing brief about this kiss. It was us coming together, with tongue and everything.

My breath was heavy by the time he pulled back.

I was halfway to hard, and I wanted nothing more than to dive back into that kiss.

But reality set in, as well as the setting.

And the *audience*.

I looked around, hoping they'd just continued along the path, but they were there waiting, both bent down and petting Nero.

"Want to walk with us?" I turned back to him, to find him looking over at Dad and Charlotte too.

He moved his focus back to me the moment I spoke.

"Where are you going?"

"Just around." I shrugged. "Probably back home once we're done with the round."

He started ahead of me, and I caught up to walk at his side. I slid my hand into his, entwining our fingers.

He glanced down, but I could tell he didn't mind, because that small, almost-there smile made an appearance again.

It had been so long since I'd seen it now. At Easter, especially, he'd been a lot happier, smiling wider, than I'd ever seen him do before.

He greeted Dad and Charlotte, who both straightened up as we joined them. Dad didn't quite look at us, so I could tell he was embarrassed.

I guess we had given them quite a show with that kiss.

Charlotte was all smiles like usual, and it didn't seem to have bothered her.

"My uncle's having a barbecue today," Jørgen said quietly once we'd started walking down the trail. "It's a gathering of family and friends. My cousin's coming back from the army, and it's to both greet him and to hang out. You should come." He cast a quick glance to the side. "All of you."

Charlotte smiled back. "We'd love to."

I looked at her in surprise, but I couldn't help smiling. I hadn't met any of Jørgen's family before, so it was both exciting and something to be nervous about.

"Nik will be there." Jørgen bumped his shoulder against mine. "Have you met Ben?"

I shook my head. "Not yet, though Nik mentions him all the time."

"You'll see them both in their full glory today, then." He grinned teasingly. If Ben was anything like Nik, it would be quite interesting. I couldn't even imagine how his best friend must be like.

"I'm looking forward to it." I brushed my free hand over his stomach, feeling the taut muscles there right under the thin vest.

He looked at me, I looked at him. His eyes darkened, and I knew mine mirrored the desire I saw there.

Why had I even worried?

I had absolutely nothing to worry about.

Jørgen still wanted me.

We would be good.

Maybe even more than good.

CHAPTER 20

"*T*his is it."

I looked up at the white-painted house with the mahogany shutters. It wasn't the biggest house in the neighbourhood, but it wasn't the smallest either. There was a driveway, with a two-car garage, a garden that stretched around the house from both sides, fenced in by a big, green hedge.

A car swung into the driveway as we stood there. I watched it curiously until a blond bloke in a green cargo uniform stepped out of the passenger seat.

I thought for a second that it was Jørgen getting out of the driver's seat, but I quickly realised that this man's hair was shorter, darker, and that he was wider over the shoulders and slightly taller. This must be the brother.

They both looked at us, and I walked ahead of
Dad and Charlotte up to greet them.

"You here for the barbecue?" the blond in the
cargo uniform asked. He was smiling disarmingly,
while the older bloke, Jørgen's brother, regarded us
in silence.

"Yeah, Jørgen invited us." That brought Jo's attention to me, and he regarded me intensely.

"Come on. We'll go around, instead of into the
house. They'll all be out back, anyway." The blond
nodded towards the side of the house on the opposite side of the garage. "I'm Andreas, by the way."

So he was the cousin coming back from the army.

It had been obvious, with the uniform, but I'd
never seen him before. He didn't look like Jørgen at
all, though he was quite handsome.

We rounded the house then, and I saw people
spread out all over the lawn. There were tables put
up, and a big grill to the side.

My gaze instantly found Jørgen sitting on a bench
in front of one of the tables. He leant back against it,
and he elbowed the black-haired bloke at his side.

The bloke turned to look at him, and when Jørgen
nodded towards us, his eyes took us in slowly before
settling on Andreas.

He was up off his seat in a second, crossing the
lawn and all but throwing himself at Andreas.

"Oh my God, you're back," I heard him murmur as his arms hooked around Andreas' neck.

"Alex," Andreas sighed. He tangled one hand in the bloke's black hair, while the other slid around his waist to pull him in closer.

I smiled at the tender moment they shared. They'd obviously missed each other a lot.

If Andreas was just back from the army, that meant he'd been gone a year. Exactly like I had.

My gaze found Jørgen again, and he looked at me instead of at them, like everyone else was. I wanted to walk over to him, but Nik was suddenly there in front of me, hugging me and kissing both my cheeks.

"There you are!" He pulled back to look at me. "Jørgen said you'd be here. This is so awesome!"

I laughed, then took in this day's vest. Considering some of the one's he'd worn before, this one wasn't so bad: *My boyfriend's hotter than your boyfriend.*

"Something you want to share?" I nodded towards his vest when he gave me a confused look.

He chuckled. "Ah, no, love. Luckily, I'm still single." His eyes cut to the side, where Alex had stepped back from Andreas. "You're looking good, Andreas. If I'd known a bloke in a uniform would be so hot, I'd consider going to the army myself."

Andreas laughed. "You, in the army? I'd like to see that."

"Wouldn't be such a good idea, would it?" Nik made a swishing movement with his wrist. "I'd be all hot on all the blokes in uniforms, wanting them to shag me and trying to grab their cocks. Bet that wouldn't go over well."

Andreas chuckled. "That wouldn't go over well at all. They were all sadly straight." Andreas didn't seem so sad about it, and neither did Alex. He kept smiling a soft, sweet smile, and his eyes never left his boyfriend. It was actually quite endearing to watch.

"I'd do you in a heartbeat." Nik winked at him and cocked his hip out.

Andreas laughed out loud again. "Too bad for you I'm already taken." He grabbed Alex by the neck and pulled him in for a kiss on his temple. Alex leaned into him.

"Heck, I'd bang you both." Nik winked again, with a wave of his hand.

I could tell they were both amused.

I was a bit shocked, though I really shouldn't have been. This was Nik, after all. It was just that I'd never actually seen him flirt like this with anyone before. When he hung out together in Oslo, it was normally just the two of us.

He didn't flirt with my family.

I glanced back at Dad, to gauge his reaction. He was glancing from Andreas and Alex to Nik, and he seemed a bit uncomfortable.

Two blonde women stepped up to Andreas next, and it wasn't hard to see that these two were his sisters. They were a mirror image of each other, and he was a male, more buff version of them. All three hugged tightly.

I finally went over to Jørgen, who'd remained seated at the table. "Hey." I sat down next to him on the bench, smiling at him.

"Hey." He moved his arm from the table top to the other side of my hip, resting it there.

I wanted to kiss him again, but we were surrounded by people, some of them his family. I settled on leaning in to kiss his cheek.

Nero was there in the next second, front paws on both sides of my hips and a pink tongue licking *my* cheek.

I laughed and pushed him down, but once he sat down on the grass, I bent down to rub his sides and pet him.

"Hey, boy." Looking at him sitting there, tongue out and being so happy about being petted, I found myself missing Charo so much it hurt.

I closed my eyes and sat back with a sigh as I gathered myself. Nero was still sitting in front of me when I opened them, gazing up at me with his dark eyes.

"Are you all right?" Jørgen's arm tightened around me.

I nodded. "I just—I suddenly really missed Charo. I miss having a dog."

Jørgen leaned in close, kissing my temple softly. "You can share mine. Or you can get a dog of your own. We can have all the dogs we want."

I turned to face him and I could see the sincerity in his eyes. "Being back here… I think I'm ready to accept a new dog. It doesn't feel right being back home without one. It can be Nero, he's gorgeous." I grinned down at him. "Maybe we can get a new dog later, once I've started earning money too."

"Whenever you want." And I could see he meant that.

IT WAS one of the best evenings I'd ever had.

I got to meet Jørgen's brother, his cousins, and the uncle who'd taken care of all his cousins when they'd needed him.

Ben hadn't been what I'd expected. He hadn't been as out there as Nik in colours and flamboyancy. Instead he'd been dressed all in black, with tattoo sleeves on both arms. He was just as outspoken as Nik, but he didn't have the campy mannerisms that Nik had.

Jo, Alex's brother, and Jørgen's uncle, Thomas, had been the three on the grill, with help from my dad once we'd arrived. Dad blended in nicely with them, even if he was older than them both.

There wasn't anyone there Charlotte's age either, but she hit it off with Christina and her best friend, a tall, brown-haired beauty.

Jørgen told me in a whisper that she was Tarjei's ex-girlfriend, which surprised me, because I'd assumed Tarjei was gay. He wasn't as flamboyant as his little brother, but he was pretty out there too. He was sitting at the other side of the table from us, joking with Nik and Ben. Their conversation was mostly about their sexual escapades.

"Could you lads tone it down?" Thomas whipped Ben over the head with a dish towel as he sat a plate piled high with sausages on the table. "Not everything's about sex."

"What rock are you living under?" Ben asked him, rolling his eyes. "Of course everything's about sex."

I grinned at their encounter and turned back to Jørgen. He was more tense now than he'd been earlier. I put a hand on his forearm. "Is it too much for you?"

He nodded only once, but it was enough.

"How about we sneak off for a bit? I don't think they'll miss us."

We headed into the house, as that was the place we were most likely to get some privacy.

He went straight to the sink to get a glass of water, and I jumped up on the counter to sit next to him. When he'd filled his glass, he stepped over to me and leaned between my legs as he drank.

"I like your family." I ran a hand over his shoulder, tracing the black tribal tattoo with my thumb. "They seem really close."

"They are."

"And not just your family, their friends as well. They all seem to be so comfortable here. Even with your uncle."

"Thomas is…" Jørgen rubbed at his temple. "He's taken care of Ben since he was young. He took the rest of them in when their dad died. He let Alex live here after he was bashed. He let him continue to live here when Andreas went off to the army. It's kind of what he does. He just takes them all in, whenever they need it."

"That is good of him."

"Yeah. Thomas is one of a kind. He's certainly the

only one of his brothers who's normal. He's trying his best to do what's best for everyone else."

I ran my fingers down his cheek in a caress. There was a slight prickle of stubble. "Has he done anything for you?"

Jørgen's eyes darkened, but it wasn't desire this time.

Then he told me about what had happen almost a year ago, last July: overdose.

Something twisted in my stomach.

"Why didn't you tell me this before?" I hated to think that he'd gone through something like that without telling me. He'd had his family around for the first time ever, but… what if it had gone wrong?

What would I have done without him?

"I don't like to think about it." He closed his eyes and shook his head. "I'm ashamed of it."

I cupped his face between my hands, rubbing my thumbs over his cheekbones. "Don't be. I'll be here no matter what. You don't have to be ashamed of telling me anything."

"I overdosed on antidepressants and sleep medication. It doesn't get much more pathetic than that."

I bent forward to kiss his forehead. "You were hurting. You just wanted it to stop. You shouldn't feel like that. Everything was okay in the end, and you got medication that was better suited to you. Just like I finally got epilepsy medication that works for me in *all* areas. In fact, I haven't had a seizure in over a month. I used to have like two a month, and now it's been over a month, and *nothing*." I kissed the tip of his nose next. "It all works out for the better in the end, no matter how far down one is at the start."

"That was very profound of you."

"I know, right?" I laughed, feeling a bit silly, but it was true. At least for us.

I kissed his lips then, and now he could answer my kisses too. "I hope you meant what you said at Easter," I said. "About living together. Because there's no way I'm going back with Dad tonight."

He drew me further up against him. The edge of the counter dug into my arse cheeks, but he held me pinned, so it wasn't like I was in any danger of falling.

"I meant it. You're coming home with me."

Something erupted in my chest, something happy, something ecstatic.

"Finally."

CHAPTER 21

J put my suitcase down at the foot of the bed in Jørgen's bedroom, then looked around.

The painting I'd done for Christmas of the two of us hung on the wall, like he'd told me. The smaller, framed picture stood on the nightstand, and the sight of it there choked me up. Of all the places he could've put that picture, he'd put it right next to his bed.

I turned to face him.

He stood in the doorway, looking at me, completely expressionless. He had his arms crossed over his chest, kind of in a defensive stance, but he loosened up once he got a look at my face.

He strode across the floor towards me, and then

we were kissing. He grabbed onto me and I clung to him. I sucked on his bottom lip and he sucked on my top lip, and it was the most erotic thing I'd ever experienced.

I was hard and aching, and I wanted him closer I wanted him as close as it was possible to get.

I wanted him inside me.

I dropped my hands down to slip under his vest. His stomach was flat and hard, and I ran my fingers over the treasure trail leading down into his jeans. I didn't move downwards, though that was what I wanted the most. Instead I ran my hands up, over his ribs and stomach, until I reached his chest. There was a light sprinkling of hair across it, which tickled my fingers and palm. I found his nipples and rolled both buds between my thumbs and index fingers.

His breath hitched against my mouth. His nipples were erect in no time, two nubs begging for more attention. I pulled his vest up further, until it stuck underneath his arms.

He got the hint and lifted his arms up so I could get the offending garment off of him. Once that was thrown away carelessly, my hands went right back to his nipples, rubbing them and playing with them.

I pressed myself up against him. He was taller than me, so my erection pressed against his upper thigh. I could feel that he was hard too, against my lower stomach.

"Do you want this?" I asked breathlessly.

I wanted him *so much*.

"I don't know," he said in a low voice. "Part of me does, part of me's terrified." He didn't move away from me, he stayed right where he was, us pressed together and my hands still playing with his nipples. "Have you done this before? Gone further, I mean?"

"Yes."

He pulled back and stared at me with wide eyes.

"Not with, like, a real person, though." I ran my hands down his sides. "Promise you won't laugh at me."

He frowned slightly. "I won't."

I pulled away from him and went over to open my suitcase. "Nik got me a present for my eighteenth birthday." I found the lube first, and I threw it up on the bed in hopes that we'd need it eventually. "It was so embarrassing. But I was also curious, so I tried it out. And let's just say we've been friends ever since." I turned around on my knees with the dildo in my hand.

Jørgen stared down at me, motionless. "That's what you've been using?"

"Yeah. I tried it out that one time, on my birthday,

and it was *so* good. And if it's that good with a toy, I can't even imagine how good it'll be with you."

He stared at the dildo.

I had just begun to wonder if showing him a life-like cock sex toy was too much, when his gaze switched over to me. It was dark, brimming with desire.

"Will you use that now?"

My lips parted in shock.

Now it was my turn to stare at the dildo.

"Will you do me afterwards?"

He nodded mutely.

I threw the dildo on the bed too as I straightened up and walked over to him. I wet my lips in nervousness. Knowing he wanted me to use the dildo while he watched was both exhilarating and a cause for anxiety.

He inched my T-shirt up my chest, and I lifted my hands so he could pull it all the way off.

"Let me watch you," he whispered against my lips. "I don't want to hurt you."

"It doesn't hurt," I whispered back. "It feels so good." I undid my jeans and pushed them down my thighs as far as I could reach, then I stamped my feet so they fell to a pool around my ankles, where I stepped out of them and kicked them away. I pressed myself up against him again, only wearing tight boxer briefs now.

My dick was hard, begging for attention.

I unbuttoned his jeans as well and pulled the flaps apart so his underwear was revealed. His cock strained against the material too, and it was so exhilarating to know that he desired me just as much as I did him.

If he wanted to watch me use the dildo, to make sure he wouldn't hurt me, then I'd give him that without blinking.

I kissed him one last time, sucking on his bottom lip and his tongue, before I pulled away to move onto the bed. I took off my boxers once I had my back to him. My cock bobbed free, and I stroked it a couple of times while I reached for the lube. I felt extremely self-conscious as I squeezed some out on my fingers.

Once I was on the bed, I contemplated if I should stay on my knees or if I should lie down on my back. I preferred to lie down when I prepared myself, so I flopped around to do just that, hiking my legs up and spreading them.

I moved my hand right down to my crack, spreading the lube over my hole. I knew he was watching me, but I closed my eyes, hoping that would make me relax a bit more. I'd always done this alone, and it was somehow less embarrassing then.

My breath hitched as I let my index finger breach my hole. It had been awhile since I'd done this now, because of the exams and the stress of them. Still, it felt just as good as it always did. I pushed another finger in and my body willingly accepted it. My body was used to the intrusion, so it didn't take me long to get myself all loose and ready.

Only the first few times had taken longer, but now... now it didn't take long at all.

With three fingers going in without discomfort, I reached for the lube again as well as the dildo. I squeezed a good amount out onto the flesh-like material of the toy, then put the head against my stretched hole.

I breathed deeply, my right hand wrapping around my neglected cock as my left hand, which was thankfully up to full function again, pushed the dildo into my body. It slid in, filling me up.

I had no idea how I must look to him.

Like a wanton slag, no doubt.

I wanked my cock in time with thrusting the dildo in and out. I was rarely loud when I did this, but my breathing was irregular and I moaned softly.

How could I not, right? I had a dildo, a very live-looking dildo, inside my body, nailing my gland, and a hand on my cock.

It felt so good, so wonderful, so amazing.

I'd closed my eyes again, so I didn't notice Jørgen until he leant over me.

My eyes flew open, and I stared up into his pale blue ones.

The dildo was pulled out of me and discarded who knew where.

Then he lowered himself on top of me.

I hiked my legs up further so I could wrap them around his waist.

Yes, yes, yes.

This was what I'd wanted, his weight atop me, pushing me down into the soft mattress. And—*yes, yes, yes*—his cock pushing into me.

I tilted my head back on a long, low moan as he pushed in. He wasn't as big as the dildo, but having him filling me up felt a thousand times better than the toy ever could.

Jørgen's lips attached themselves to my neck, causing another moan from me as he sucked on the thin skin.

I buried my fingers in his hair, not pulling, but holding his head down right there against the thin, sensitive skin. I didn't care if he made a mark. I wanted him to make one, to mark me.

This was the first time I'd ever been with someone like this.

It was definitely better than using a dildo.

His cock slid smoother into me than the dildo did, and the sensations were like night and day. Now I had his weight atop me, his thighs against the back of mine, his balls slapping against my crack, the smell of his cologne and his sweat surrounding me.

It was heaven.

Jørgen lifted his head, and I didn't even try to push him back down towards my neck, because he kissed me and that was certainly the more preferable option. It was a close second, though. His lips against mine, his tongue pushing between my lips. His body rocking against mine. It was all so erotic.

Though I'd let go off my cock, it wasn't forgotten.

Jørgen's stomach rubbed against it on each stroke of his hips, the coarse hair of his treasure trail teasing the sensitive head.

I could come like this, with his cock thrusting into me, his body teasing my cock to completion, and with his lips on mine.

I whimpered—*whimpered*—as I shot between us in several short squirts. I could feel the warm, sticky semen settle on my stomach, in my bellybutton, but most of all I could feel his cock nailing my prostate on *every* thrust.

My cock let out a couple of new quick squirts, causing yet another whimper to escape me.

His breathing turned erratic as well, and he groaned as he did several slower, deeper thrusts into me. I could tell he was coming from the change in pace, and I clung to his hair as he came inside me.

I could feel some of the semen trickle out and down my crack as he thrust a few times more.

He collapsed atop me and I wrapped my arms around his shoulders. His skin had a sheen of sweat on it, and I knew mine had as well. Sex was a sweaty, messy affair, but I didn't care at all. Because he was lying atop me, his spent cock was inside me, his semen was inside me. Because we'd got as close as two people could ever get and it felt wonderful.

I stroked one hand over his shoulder blades, over the tattoo. For the first time ever I could see the whole thing, and it went over both shoulders and down over his spine, about halfway down his back.

Once his breathing calmed a bit, he rolled off me.

He moved onto his stomach, elbows propped up and his face buried in his palms.

I watched him quietly, gauging his mood. When he only stayed like that, breathing calmly, I rolled over onto my side.

"Jørgen?" I put my hand on his shoulder,

brushing it over his still sweat-slick skin. "Are you all right?"

He sighed deeply, but stayed in that position. I moved my hand up to tangle in the short hairs in his neck.

"Didn't you like it, what we did?" He must've liked it; he'd come, after all. I could still feel a small trickle of semen run down from my hole.

My arse felt it too. I wasn't sore, not really, but I could certainly feel that I'd been fucked.

I liked that feeling.

I liked it a lot.

And I hoped he had too, that what we'd just done hadn't pulled him right into a flashback, that this wouldn't lead to a panic attack...

"Jørgen?"

Please be okay.

But when he didn't answer, but stomach sank. Disappointment and guilt warred inside me.

I'd pushed this on him—and it had been too soon. He'd been doing so good, but now, because of me, he'd taken several steps backwards.

I bit my lip and squeezed my eyes shut.

Shit.

CHAPTER 22

"You didn't like it, did you?"

I felt hollow inside.

"I did." He lifted his head out of his hands and turned to look at me. "I did, Geir. Was it good for you?"

I blinked, surprised, then the warm, post-orgasmic feeling of bliss crept back into me.

"Oh yeah," I sighed dreamily. "It was amazing."

"I don't think I could *ever* be in the position you were in. Not even with you. I can't give you that." His voice broke at the end.

It clicked instantly for me.

"Of course not, Jørgen. With your past—I would never expect that. Being on top... that hasn't even occurred to me. I like being the bottom. I like having your weight on me, pressing me down, having you inside me. No, I don't like it, even, I *love* it. It's so intimate, we're so close and I just—" I shook my head. I didn't have words to describe what it was like. "I love you."

He didn't answer, but the sudden bright light in his eyes told me everything I needed to know.

I bent forward to kiss him. He rolled onto his back in the middle of the kiss so he could get his hands on me. I crawled onto his lap, settling my bum against his flaccid cock.

Mine was already hardening again, ready for another round. The smattering of hair on his thighs tickled my arse cheeks as I switched between rubbing back against the front of his thighs and down against his cock.

Our kiss was slow and lazy, only lips sliding against lips.

"You need to tell me if any of this makes you uncomfortable," I whispered against his lips. "I won't be hurt. I'll just be careful not to do it again. I want you to trust me completely."

"I do. I do trust you completely." He opened his eyes to gaze up at me. "I just, I can't ever let you do me."

"That's okay." I grinned against his lips. "Because I have no desire for our roles to be switched. I know a lot of men are versatile, but that others aren't. You're only comfortable topping, and that's perfectly okay with me, because I rather like being the bottom." His cock hardened again under me, and I lifted myself up so I could look down on him. "I've never seen you naked before. In fact, I hadn't even seen you without a shirt before today."

His body was toned. Not overly muscular, like the blokes that constantly lifted weights, but the muscles were there right under his skin. His chest had a smattering of hair, darker than the hair on his head. The same colour as his stubble. His stomach was flat, with a treasure trail leading down to a long, thick cock surrounded by short, coarse pubic hair. His balls were tight, nestled nicely between his spread legs. His legs too had a smattering of hair, but there wasn't too much of it.

It was a stark contrast to me, though, who hardly had any body hair at all. I wondered if I was just slow at growing it, if it would make its appearance later, or if I would be mostly hairless for the rest of my life.

My arms were braced next to Jørgen's head, but I moved one hand down to cup his balls, rolling them between my fingers. I'd only ever touched myself before, and touching him was so very different. Both my cock and balls were smaller than his.

I wrapped my fingers around his hard cock next. It was still slick from lube and come, and my hand glided over the tender skin easily. I pulled the foreskin up, hiding the mushroom-shaped head from view, then stroked back down to reveal it in all its pink-slick glory.

I debated with myself if I wanted to try sucking him off or if I wanted him inside of me again.

The latter won.

"Can I ride you?" I looked up at him. His eyes were glazed over and halfway closed as he gazed down at me touching him.

"If you want."

I grinned wickedly. "Oh, I want."

I sat up so I could position myself properly, then I held onto the base of his cock as I lowered myself onto it. I was stretched and lubed from before, so he slid in all the way easily.

A moan left me as my arse settled on his lap, because the head was already rubbing against that special gland inside me.

I bent forward to kiss him, with him still buried balls deep inside me. It was a quick kiss, because I needed to move and I wasn't sure I could focus on both things at once.

His hands settled on my thighs as I started humping up and down on him.

My cock, still erect, bounced freely. I could see him staring at it, but he didn't do anything. Only his hands clenched tighter on my thighs.

I took one of his hands in mine and put it around my cock. "You can touch me all you want," I gasped out. "Please."

And he did. He wanked me off while I fucked myself on his cock.

It didn't take me long to orgasm again, with the double pleasure of him inside me and his big, calloused hand around me.

I cried out as I shot onto his stomach in several quick, small spurts. Some trickled down over his hand, but he kept on stroking me until I was completely spent.

I ground myself down on his lap, loving the full feeling of him inside me, but after coming twice I felt too sensitive to continue riding him. When I rose back up, I let him slip out. His cock dropped back onto his stomach, still hard and straining.

I licked my lips as I stared at it. I wanted to lick it, suck it, to feel it in my mouth and against my tongue.

But we'd just had bareback sex.

The thought of doing so now squicked me out.

My gaze rose further up his body. His nipples were there, puckered and all but begging to be played with. I bent over to suck one in, while my hand wrapped around his straining dick.

I'd wank him off for now.

I could taste him later.

"Oh fuck. Geir." One of his hands tangled in my hair, but he didn't push me away.

Hearing his voice like that, so deep and hoarse and filled with lust—it was amazing.

Back when we'd met, this wouldn't have been possible.

And now here we were, having *sex*.

No, making love.

I'd been dreaming of being with him like this ever since my sex drive had surfaced, and especially after our little tryst at Easter. It had been just a little taste of what was to come and it had made me want so much more. It was to the thought of him that always got me off, when I wanked off or used the dildo.

"I'm coming," he warned me, pulling slightly on my hair to get my attention.

I pulled back from his nipple, but continued to stroke him, as I wanted to see his face, and his cock, when he came.

No!

I wanted to taste him.

Moving downwards, I stuck my tongue out, anticipation coursing through me at what was to come.

This, too, was something I'd never done before.

The first shot landed on my cheek, and I tilted my head a bit so the next squirt did land on my tongue.

Mmm, salty.

The next trickled down from the slit and over my fingers, but the last landed on my tongue too.

I moved up to lie next to him when he was milked dry. I turned his head to look at me, then grinned. He reached up and wiped the semen that had landed on my cheek off, which caused me to blush as I had completely forgotten about it.

Then I decided *to hell with with* and I grabbed his hand, sucked his fingers into my mouth, and licked the semen off of them.

"You said I'd changed. But I think you've changed most of all," I said once we were back to resting peacefully next to each other. "Last year this wouldn't even be a possibility, and yet look at us now."

"It wasn't for you either."

"No, but that's because of my medication. A simple change of dosage would've changed it, like it did when I finally went to see my doctor in Oslo. But you've come so far since last year, Jørgen. Farther than I've come."

He was silent for so long I didn't think he'd say anything else on the matter.

"I've never done this before. Every time I was… forced… it was all about him and not about me. He invaded my body, took his pleasure any way he could get it. I never knew it could be like this. So pure and intimate. So *good*. I never thought I'd have this with anyone, ever.

"And then you came along and proved it all wrong. You proved I could fall for someone. That I could love. You proved that I can give everything in a relationship when I didn't think I could ever be enough."

"You are more than enough." I put my hand on his stomach, forgetting how sticky he was from my come. I swirled my finger around in it, the simple thought of him covered in my come was enough to excite me again.

I couldn't get it up anytime soon, or come again, but the thought was still there and it wasn't going away.

"You have been, since the beginning, even if you scared me sometimes. Not like I was afraid of you, but in that I didn't know what to do for you to make you feel better."

He took my hand in his, twining our fingers together, semen and all. "It was enough for you just to be there."

"I will always be there for you, no matter what."

He turned his head to look at me again. His face was neutral, but his eyes were intense.

"You're here now. For good. You're not going anywhere."

"No," I said. "I'm not."

WE SHOWERED, changed the sheets, then fell back into bed in a tangle.

We slept entwined most of that night.

I didn't think either of us wanted to let the other go in case we woke up and it was all a dream.

At least, that was what I was afraid of, and I was pretty sure that was the reason he held onto me too.

He even managed to sleep through the whole night without waking, at least as far as I could tell, and I woke up first that morning.

His arms weren't around me now, though he was lying close to my back.

I inched out of bed, as quietly as possible so I wouldn't disturb him. I took the first and best joggers out of my suitcase on my way past it, then I slipped out into the living room and over to the kitchen.

I wanted to make him breakfast. Breakfast we could enjoy in bed.

The fridge was better stocked than it had been

back when I'd visited for the autumn holiday. I pulled out butter and eggs and bacon, then checked if he had bread. He didn't, but that didn't matter. I'd just make an English breakfast instead. I fried the eggs in the big frying pan, and found a smaller one to fry the bacon in.

He had sausages in the fridge too, and I took them out. He didn't like mushrooms, and neither did I, so I skipped those.

Did he like beans?

I wasn't sure, but I couldn't stand them, so I left them out as well.

Half an English breakfast was still a breakfast, right?

There was one thing on an English breakfast I was sorely missing, the hash browns. I'd only tasted them once, but they'd been good. I had no idea how to make them, so eggs, bacon, and sausage it would have to be.

I poured us each a glass of orange juice, and as I put all on a small tray I found in one of the cupboards, Nero came padding into the kitchen.

I greeted him in a whisper, afraid to make a sound in case Jørgen woke up before I could surprise him in bed. I filled Nero's food, changed his water, then told him to stay as I hoisted the tray and made my way back to the bedroom.

Jørgen hadn't moved from the position I'd left him in. The duvet pooled around his waist, showing off his magnificent back with that stark, black tattoo. Only when I put my knee on the mattress did he stir, and he rolled over onto his back as he stretched his arms above his head.

"Morning." I smiled down at him and he blinked up at me groggily.

"You're up?" he asked, surprised. He eyed the tray in my hand, and his confusion grew. "I didn't hear you get out of bed."

"I was rather quiet. It was very stealthy, really." I settled next to him, leaning back against the headboard. "I think our activities last night wore you out, and that's why you didn't even move a muscle when I got out of bed."

He stared up at me, then pushed himself up so he could sit next to me.

The duvet fell further down to pool in his lap. It was thin, not a thick one like he'd used last autumn, and as he was naked I could clearly see the outline of his cock through the fabric.

I licked my lips as my excitement grew, but this morning wasn't about sex. It was about me making him breakfast and us enjoying it in bed.

"Here. I made us an English breakfast."

I put the tray on his lap, then lifted his duvet so I

could sit under it as well. I was still wearing my joggers, but I had nothing on underneath them or on my feet, so I was feeling a bit chilly.

"Not a proper one, it's missing half of what makes it an English breakfast, but still. I was going to make us fried eggs and bacon, and put it on bread, but you didn't have any, so this is what happened."

He put an arm around my shoulders, and I leaned in so he could kiss my temple. "Thanks. This looks delicious."

We didn't speak as we ate.

We did, however, enjoy the food. It was still warm and it was delicious. Not the healthiest breakfast, certainly, or the most substantial, but delicious all the same.

When we were done, I bent over to put the tray down on the floor, then I curled up against him. His arms were instantly around me again, and I tilted my head up for a kiss.

I scooted around so I could lie down flat on my back. I drew him with me, not breaking our kiss, and he propped his forearms next to my head so he wouldn't put his entire body weight on me.

I regretted not taking off my joggers before I got into the bed, because he was all naked against me.

In fact, why had I even put them on?

I was in his flat, it was only the two of us here,

and no one else to see us. I could've made breakfast in the nude.

He rocked against me.

It wasn't the frenzy of the night before.

It was slow, and loving, like he had all the time in the world.

And we did now, didn't we? I was *home*. I was with him. No more living in Oslo for a year, no more only seeing him during holidays.

There would be no more missing him, because I would get to see him every day from now on. I'd wake up next to him every morning. No more talking on the phone, or writing letters, because we were finally together.

Where we should be, where we belonged.

"Take my joggers off," I whispered against his lips. "I want to feel you without anything in the way."

We managed to get the garment off without breaking too much contact between us. I threw the joggers away over my head, hoping they didn't land on the breakfast tray. We might've finished breakfast, but the plates were covered in grease.

When he lowered himself between my thighs again, we were both gloriously naked. Our cocks lined up, rocking together slowly. He didn't increase his rhythm, and I wasn't about to ruin the tender moment we shared by bucking up against him. This was good, exactly as it was.

"I love you so much."

I almost didn't catch it, because his voice was so low, but I did. I wrapped my arms around him, burying my hands in his hair as we rocked together in that torturously slow rhythm.

"More than anything, Geir. I love you."

My breath caught in my throat, even if he'd said it to me before.

This moment, right here, was so different from the other times he'd said it. We were as close as we'd ever been now, lying there in bed naked and rocking together. It wasn't about getting off, it was simply about feeling good, about feeling close to each other.

About loving each other.

My voice shook as I answered him. "I love you too. More than you'll ever know."

And we continued to rock together—because we had all the time in the world.

ABOUT THE AUTHOR

TT lives in Norway and writes about gay men living in Norway. She also occasionally writes about gay men living in the UK, because she loves the UK. Norway might be too cold for her, but TT doesn't like the summer, so she's learned to adapt. TT is happiest in front of her computer, creating emotional stories about men loving other men.

www.ttkove.com
ttkove@gmail.com